THE SHADOWMAN'S WAY

Other Avon Camelot Books by
Paul Pitts

RACING THE SUN

Until recently, Paul Pitts and his wife Kathleen lived on a Navajo Indian reservation in southeastern Utah. Mr. Pitts and his wife now live in Sandy, Utah where he is active in the Utah Writing Project. *The Shadowman's Way* is Paul Pitt's third book for young people.

THE SHADOWMAN'S WAY

PAUL PITTS

AN AVON CAMELOT BOOK

THE SHADOWMAN'S WAY is an original publication of Avon Books. This work has never before appeared in book form.

AVON BOOKS
A division of
The Hearst Corporation
1350 Avenue of the Americas
New York, New York 10019

Copyright © 1992 by Paul Pitts
Published by arrangement with the author
Library of Congress Catalog Card Number: 91-92459
ISBN: 0-380-76210-2
RL: 5.0

First Avon Camelot Printing: May 1992

CAMELOT TRADEMARK REG. U.S. PAT. OFF. AND IN OTHER COUNTRIES, MARCA REGIS-TRADA, HECHO EN U.S.A.

Printed in the U.S.A.

OPM   10 9 8 7 6 5 4 3 2

With
love and appreciation

For
the people of Montezuma Creek,
more than friends,
they're family

and

For
De Ann Forbes,
who reads with her scissors ready

Chapter One

Without opening my eyes, I knew Anson was standing next to the bed. The smell of peanuts nudged me awake.

"Mom says you have to get up right now." The peanut smell grew stronger. "You're going to be late." Every day for the entire nine years of his life, my little brother has had peanut butter and honey on toast for breakfast.

"She says I can get you up any way I want," he said, smugly.

I turned to lie on my stomach and burrowed into the pillow, holding my blankets tight in case he tried to pull them off. "I'm awake, Anson. You've done your job. Now leave me alone."

"She didn't say *wake* up, Nelson, she said *get* up." A few drops of water splattered on the back of my neck and slid down toward my chin.

Rolling to my back, I opened my eyes to catch another dribble of water. As I kicked my legs over the side of the bed, Anson jumped back. He was holding my Garfield cup.

"Look, elephant breath, I'm up. Satisfied?"

"Get all the way out of bed first."

I tried to glare at him but it took too much energy. I'm not a natural glarer, especially first thing in the morning.

1

The water torture was my own fault. The night before, I'd left my art materials out on the desk after working on a watercolor. I should follow my mother's advice and put things away right after I finish with them.

I stood up and waited for Anson to set the cup down. "Cheyennes tie annoying little brothers on ant hills and pour honey over them."

He grinned. "We're not Cheyennes, we're Navajos."

"I'm not against borrowing good ideas from other cultures." I straightened my pillow and pulled the covers over it. If I don't make my bed as soon as I get up, it doesn't get made, and Mom gets mad.

"Anyway, we're out of honey. I ate the last of it for breakfast."

My brother's bed was already made in his unique, lumpy way. We share the room and he insists on having the top bunk. It gives him an excuse for having rumpled blankets and a crooked bedspread.

"Have you seen my math book, Nelson? I have to finish my homework." He always waits till the last minute.

"No." I started putting away my art materials. "But if you'd organize your stuff, you'd be able to find things."

"I think I left it up here." He searched under the pile of clean underwear on top of the chest of drawers.

"Mom told you to put your clothes away."

"I did." He dropped to the floor and looked under the bed.

"*Put away* means in your drawer, not on top," I said.

Grabbing the stack of shorts, he pulled his drawer out and paused. "Here it is." He grabbed the math book, threw the underwear into the drawer and slammed it.

"I want to be early today," he said. "There's a new kid in town, a *Bilagaana*. He's in fourth grade."

2

"How do you know?" I was flipping through the shirts hanging on my side of the closet.

"He told me. His dad's going to run Gas and Goodies. They moved in yesterday. If you weren't hanging around the river all the time, you'd have seen the moving van."

"It's dangerous to talk to strangers."

"He's not a stranger, just a kid. I was watching the men carry chairs and stuff and he came over and said, 'My name's David, what's yours?' "

Anson walked over and sat on my bed. "He's got a big brother, too, a high school kid."

I grabbed my Broncos tee-shirt. "If they just moved in, your buddy probably won't be in school today. He'll wait a few days to get settled."

He was trying to smooth out his wrinkled math paper. "Have you got a pencil, Nelson?"

"When are you going to start developing some respon . . ." As he sighed and looked at the ceiling, a picture of me four years earlier flashed into my mind. When I was in fourth grade, Russell gave me the same lecture every day and I hated it. I pulled out the desk drawer and found a couple of eraserless stubbs. "Here."

"Wow! These are great. Are you sure you can spare them? I hate to take your best pencils."

He's spoiled and annoying but I can't stay mad at him. I found a new pencil and tossed it over.

"Try to hang onto it till school starts."

"If I super-glue it to my hand, it might last till noon." He laughed.

At lunch, as I stared down at the blob on my tray, I got the strangest feeling that it was staring back.

Let's hear a cheer for school lunch, I thought. Another entry for the 'Food Poisoning Hall of Fame.' I poked what

3

I hoped was a black olive back into the cheese, noodles and tomato sauce.

In a high school with only four hundred students in all six grades, it should be easy to provide nourishing, tasty lunches. But we seem to get more than our share of *mystery meals*. The problem might be that Carson's Crossing is in the middle of nowhere, but it also might have something to do with the fact that most of the students are Navajo.

I can hear the members of the state school board discussing it. "Those kids will eat anything. What do they know about real food anyway?"

I knew that inspectors from the state health department come around to check up now and then, still. . . . I decided not to take a chance on the main dish. Canned peaches and milk would have to do.

Benjamin Nez and his friends were at the third table, so I sat at the second one. I didn't want them to think I was avoiding them but I didn't want to be in on their conversation either. As usual, they didn't even notice.

I might as well tell you right now that I'm one guy who gets along with everyone. That's because no one knows I'm around most of the time. I'm a shadowman. If you took a poll and asked, "What do you think of Nelson Sam?", people would say, "Who?" I have that kind of personality. I don't have a million friends, but I don't make enemies either. I just blend in with the scenery.

As I reached for my milk carton, I glanced across the tables at Benjamin. In Navajo, the name *Nez* means *tall*, but Benjamin's body hadn't caught on to that. He wasn't much taller than me, even though he was held back in third grade. Since then we've gone all through school together.

Manuelito High goes from seventh to twelfth grade. If

we were in a real school, like they have in town, we'd be in junior high, mighty eighth graders, the high men on the totem pole. That's an Indian joke. Instead, we're middle men.

When they named the school Manuelito, after the Navajo chief, they were "preserving the heritage of our Native American students." That's what the school board president said at the dedication of the building.

Preserving heritage is very important to Benjamin Nez. He works hard at being Navajo. He even pulls out the few whiskers he has with tweezers, just like old-time Navajos used to do instead of shaving. He doesn't pull out the mustache hair but you can't tell that unless you look real close. It grows down around the ends of his lips with nothing under his nose. I know he's proud of it anyway. I see him smoothing it down every time he passes the mirror in the boys' room.

Benjamin's friends were all sitting around him at the third table. There was Freeman Tom and Johnny Begay who wears one turquoise earring. Cecil Benally was next and then Alex Begay. Alex and Johnny aren't brothers—Begay is a common name for Navajos. Freeman is Benjamin's best friend. He'd pull out his whiskers with tweezers too, if he had any.

"The thing that makes me mad," Benjamin's voice floated across the cafeteria, "is the way they push us around."

He stroked his imaginary mustache. "The whites forced us onto land that nobody else wanted. Then, when they discovered oil and uranium, they moved in, drilling wherever they wanted, ruining the roads, cheating our people out of their mineral rights. . . ."

The conversation was on Benjamin's favorite subject.

5

"We should just kick every last one of them off the reservation. Navajo land should be for Navajos."

It's a familiar speech. I shared some of his ideas with my dad once when we were fixing our old pickup.

"What do you think?" I asked, handing him a screwdriver.

"I think I asked for a half-inch wrench."

"Sorry." I exchanged the tool. "I mean, do you think *Bilagaanas* have pushed us around?"

"Yep, but spending all your time complaining about it doesn't do much good."

He was quiet while he worked on a rusty nut. I thought that was all he had to say on the subject.

Then he straightened up and looked at me. "This may be land that nobody else wanted, but Navajos wanted it. If the government would've offered us a choice of any place to live in the whole country, we would've chosen here. This is our home."

He wiped his hands on a greasy, orange rag. "It's true that some people sold their mineral rights for what amounted to pocket change for the big companies. It seemed like a fortune because the people didn't know any better." He tried to loosen the stubborn nut again, but continued talking. "You change that kind of cheating by educating people, not complaining."

"What about kicking whites out of town?"

He grinned. "In the first place, I don't think our feet are big enough. In the second place, if they go, they take the jobs with them. We aren't ready to run drilling companies, refineries, things like that. So we're back to education again." With a screech, the nut gave up. My dad twisted it off the bolt. "We've got some small businesses started; we're moving in the right direction."

My father had never talked so much at one time.

"One last thing." He wasn't finished. "Thinking all whites are bad because some of them cheat is foolish. At the refinery there are all kinds of men. Before I quit working there and took over this station, I knew them all. I knew Pete Yazzie, not a *Navajo,* and Don Willard, not a *Bilagaana.* Some whites never got past thinking of me as an *Indian,* but there were Navajos who were the same way with *Bilagaanas.* It's best to work side-by-side with friends, no matter what they look like."

Whenever Benjamin starts his *Navajo land for Navajos* speech, I think of what my dad said.

The instructions on a milk carton seem so simple: To Open—Pull Here. As usual, I had to use my spoon to pry it open.

Benjamin was still talking. "What have the whites given us?" The others knew that he'd answer his own question, all they had to do was listen. "Nothing!" he finally spit out. "They take everything and they give us nothing."

Actually, that's not quite true. We really don't have it so bad. The government pays all our school fees. We have free hospitals and dental clinics. If we want to go out for a sport or on a field trip or take an art class, all expenses are paid. We even get free school lunch. Considering the blob on my tray, that might be counted a plus or a minus. Anyway, Benjamin was wearing Levis and cowboy boots from Penney's, so I wasn't convinced that whites hadn't made some contribution to his life. If he really wanted to make his point, he'd be wearing a loincloth and moccasins.

I was trying to cut up my peaches without looking at the blob when everything got quiet. Such silence has only happened once this year. Last fall a kid ran into Mrs.

Johnson and slammed her full lunch tray against her new start-the-school-year dress. Everyone waited to hear her scream and get mad, but she didn't. She just stood quietly with spaghetti sliding down her front and waited for one of the cooks to bring a dishcloth. Mrs. Johnson teaches social studies. She spends a lot of time telling students to "hold fast to your inner strength." Her favorite line is, "You have the power to act upon your environment rather than reacting to it!" I guess she was showing us what that means.

In today's silence, every kid seemed to be looking past me so I turned around to see what was going on. Mr. Carpenter, the principal, had just come in with a new student. New students aren't all that rare at Manuelito. Navajos move around a lot, but this kid was white. There are only about twenty white students in the whole school.

This must be the kid Anson was talking about, I thought.

It was so quiet you could hear old Carpenter giving the new kid a grand tour. He showed him the lunch line, telling him about our talented cooks. When they got to the main dish, even Carpenter couldn't figure out what it was. He stopped talking for a minute. Finally he wished the new kid "good luck" and walked away.

The boy was a little taller than me. He had on slacks and a long-sleeved dress shirt instead of jeans and a tee-shirt. His hair was light brown and he had freckles. The strangest thing about him was the way he was smiling at everybody. He even said "Thank you" to the cooks. Then he started toward the lunch tables and I turned back to scoop up my peaches. It's hard enough being new in school without everyone staring at you.

The silence made me nervous and I looked up. Every-one on Benjamin's table was looking in my direction.

8

A throat was cleared. "Mind if I sit here?"

The new kid was standing right beside me. Me, Nelson Sam—the world's champion at avoiding spotlights!

What could I say? I just mumbled, "Okay," and went on eating. I could feel Benjamin's eyes staring a hole in the top of my head but I didn't look up.

"My name's Spencer West," the kid said. "Everybody calls me 'Spence.' "

"Hi," I whispered, keeping my head down.

"What's yours?"

"Nelson . . ." I paused. ". . . Sam." I glanced over at the next table. Freeman was elbowing Benjamin and they were laughing.

"We just moved into town. We're going to run the store, Gas and Goodies." He shook his head. "What a dumb name. It's a franchise. There's dozens of those places around the country, maybe hundreds." He laughed. "Picture it, Sam, somewhere there's a tall, dignified home office building with *Gas and Goodies* written on it."

This kid thought my *first* name was Sam. I should have set him straight, but I didn't want to talk any more than I had to. I could feel Benjamin and his friends checking to see if I was buddying up with *Mr. Dress Shirt*.

"It's not my problem," the kid went on. "If my dad's ego can survive being manager of Gas and Goodies, why should I complain?" He was opening his milk, destroying the carton just like I'd done. "At least it's better than running that dumpy Texaco station."

I didn't look at him. "My dad runs the dumpy Texaco station."

After a few seconds of silence, he mumbled, "Sorry. It's not really that bad. Probably it's a lot better on the inside."

"It's not, it's even dumpier."

9

Silence again.

Keeping my head down to hide my lips from Benjamin's table, I continued. "We just don't have time to fix it up like the Gas and Goodies showcase. We're too busy taking care of the customers that drive right by your shiny new store."

The new kid was quiet. Then he noticed I was smiling.

He laughed. "My dad's not really a mechanic anyway. I guess you have to be a mechanic to run a place like yours."

I nodded but kept my eyes focused on my tray. I was running out of things to eat so I pretended to drink from my empty milk carton.

"So . . . tell me about Manuelito High School, Sam." He seemed to be working to keep the conversation going. In class I've noticed that it's important to the white kids to keep talking. It's different with Navajos, we like silence. If there's a pause in the talking, it's not uncomfortable for us.

"Manuelito's okay . . . It's just a school," I said.

Benjamin called to me in Navajo. "Nelson, did your dog follow you to school today?"

Even though I was sure the new kid couldn't understand what he said, I was embarrassed for him.

"Is he talking to you?" the kid asked.

"He says it's different to have a new student here."

The kid smiled and raised his voice so Benjamin could hear. "Hi, my name's Spence West. My dad's going to run Gas and Goodies."

Benjamin stood up slowly and came over to us. As he sat down on the other side of the table, students moved up to stand behind him, an audience for lunchtime entertainment.

Benjamin's grin was an inch too wide. "I just want

you to know that we feel very privileged to have another *Bilagaana* in our school."

"*Bilagaana?*" the kid asked.

"A white man," Benjamin explained.

"*Bilagaana*, I'll have to remember that," Spencer said. "I'm going to try to learn some Navajo. It might help me wait on customers in the store."

The grin faded and a cold look froze across Benjamin's face. "There are a couple of people around here that speak English."

The white kid blushed. "No offense. I just thought it would be great to learn Navajo."

Benjamin smiled again. "I can teach you a few things if you want. For a start, when you say 'Hello' to someone, you say, *'Ya'at'eeh, kl'izi sani.'* "

When the new kid repeated it, a few observers started giggling.

"I guess it's going to take time to learn the right pronunciation," he said and laughed with them.

I couldn't think of a quiet way to let him know that he was making a fool of himself.

"After you say 'Hello,' " Benjamin continued, "you ought to introduce yourself. Say, *'Dibe bichaan Bilagaana bith thlikaan.'* "

This time the kids really laughed.

The dumb kid kept repeating the phrase until even the cooks were laughing.

Finally, I stood up and went to dump my tray.

"Wait up, Sam," the new kid called, following me.

An old Navajo man coming in the door asked me what was on the lunch menu. I couldn't think of a way to describe it in English, let alone Navajo. "What would you call that main dish?" I asked the new kid.

"Is he going to eat that stuff?"

11

I shrugged. "Probably. Community people, especially older ones, are given lunch if they drop by at noon. It's sort of a cultural, Navajo-hospitality thing."

"Just tell him about the peaches," the kid suggested.

I did. No use spoiling his appetite before he actually looked at his tray.

"I might as well try out the Navajo I learned," Spencer West said.

"Maybe I ought to explain. . . ." I started but he was already talking.

"*Ya'at'eeh, kl'izi sani,*" he said.

The old man looked puzzled.

"*Dibe bichaan Bilagaana bith thlikaan,*" Spencer finished.

The old man shook his head and walked on, chuckling.

"Didn't I say it right?" Spencer asked when we got out in the hall.

"You said it perfectly." I had to smile. "There was no way he could misunderstand that you called him an old goat and told him that white men like to eat sheep droppings."

He stopped. "I what?"

I explained. " '*Kl'izi sani*' means old goat and the rest says that sheep manure is really tasty to white men."

"Oh, no!" He clamped his hands against his head. "What a dope!"

"No argument about that from me." I walked faster, hoping to lose the dope in the crowd.

Chapter Two

Weaving through the students milling around in the hall, I reminded myself for the hundredth time that I didn't need a new friend, especially a *Bilagaana*. The kid was friendly and he had a good sense of humor and I felt sorry for him, coming into a new school at the end of the year, but I was busy enough just keeping myself out of trouble.

"Hey, Sam!" The noise in the hallway stopped as everyone turned to watch the crazy white kid chase me. "Wait a minute, will you?"

I slowed down. It would be less conspicuous to walk with him than have him shouting at me.

"Where's the fire?" he said, coming up beside me.

I didn't answer and we walked in silence for almost a minute. Then, I led him into the library.

I'd decided to take the time to set him straight about the way things work at Manuelito High and this was a good empty room to talk in. Ms. Benally keeps the library open at lunch but she insists that students read quietly or study. Who wants to spend free time doing those things?

I chose a table near the window. "Sit down."

"Yes, sir," he said obediently.

When I saw Ms. Benally looking at us from her office

window, I went over to the shelf and got a couple of books. I laid one in front of the new kid, sat down, and opened the other to pretend I was reading.

He glanced around. "Wow! This is really something! I've never seen a school library with all this stuff: records, video tapes, beanbag chairs, study carrels, a weaving loom in the corner. . . ."

In spite of my mood, I enjoyed his enthusiasm. It was almost as though I'd had something to do with designing the library.

"Schools on the reservation get money from different programs," I said. "We have grants from the federal government and some from the state. The Navajo Tribe even gave us money to use for books and library stuff."

He looked out through the floor-length windows to the small plaza in the middle of the school.

"That patio is nice," he said.

"It's all right first thing in the morning but this time of day, it's like an oven."

"They should plant some shade trees," Spence said.

"What do you think those sticks by the benches are?"

"Oh." He smiled. "I didn't recognize them. I guess I'm used to trees with branches and leaves."

"Give them time. The school was just built last year."

There was a minute of silence, then I cleared my throat and he looked over.

"I didn't bring you in here to discuss landscape gardening," I started. "I just want to give you a little information."

"Information?"

"You need to know about Benjamin Nez." I shrugged. "So you can stay out of trouble."

"Trouble?" There was a definite echo in the library.

14

"Benjamin and the rest of those kids don't like Anglos very much."

"Anglos?"

"Whites . . . *Bilagaanas.*" I pushed on to get the explanation over before the bell rang. "They usually just stay to themselves, but they'll give the white kids a bad time if they get the chance."

"You mean like teaching us Navajo?" He smiled.

"Only the ones who are crazy enough to repeat what they say."

He laughed. It was so honest, I couldn't help myself. I joined in.

Just then Benjamin and Freeman walked out the door onto the bright patio. I flinched a little.

"Speaking of my Navajo language teacher . . ." He stood up. "Maybe we ought to move back from the window so they won't see us talking."

This kid was smarter than he'd let on in the lunchroom.

"The windows have some kind of reflective coating," I told him. "You can see out but they can't see in. It's supposed to keep the building cooler."

He sat down again. "What I can't figure out is how those guys can dislike me already. They don't even know me."

"They know you're white and that's all they want to know. Around here whites mostly hang around with whites and Navajo kids stay with Navajos."

"How about you?"

"I'm a loner. I just stay to myself."

"But if we become friends . . ."

"We won't," I said. I could see I'd have to put it to him stronger. "I like being a loner and I don't want any trouble from Benjamin and his group."

He just looked at me.

15

"You mean," he said at last, "that your friendship with Benjamin would keep you from having a white friend?"

Maybe he wasn't as smart as I'd thought. "I don't have a friendship with Benjamin and his buddies." The chair squeaked as I shifted my weight. "They don't even know I'm around. But, if I had a white friend, they'd notice me and then I'd become a target for their hassling, too."

It was really quiet for a few seconds. Then Spencer spoke again.

"The setup here at school seems like a dumb way of running things. I'm an Army brat. My dad dragged the whole family all over the place so I've been in lots of different schools that were made up of students from different cultures." He offered me a stick of gum. While I unwrapped it, he went on. "Why doesn't the school start some programs or clubs or something, so that kids from different backgrounds can get to know each other?"

"They tried that. Mr. Carpenter started an Indian Club at the first of the year. Mr. Toledo, the art teacher, was the sponsor. He's my favorite teacher so I went to the first few meetings.

"Carpenter announced a special invitation to the white kids but I guess they were too shy to show up, maybe they just weren't interested. The plan was for us to learn about Navajo history, even traditional songs and dances. Mr. Toledo was willing to learn how to read and write Navajo so he could teach us."

"You mean you don't know how to read Navajo?" Spencer said.

"I don't know anyone who does. Like most Indian languages, it wasn't written down, just passed along orally. Missionaries worked at preserving it in writing but it took World War II to show how valuable a written Indian language might be."

"World War II?"

I nodded. "They used Navajos to send messages in their own language. It drove the enemy crazy, trying to figure out the code."

Outside the window, Benjamin and Freeman were wrestling around, trying to push one another into a barren flower bed.

"Anyway, with Benjamin there, the Indian Club turned into a gripe session about whites abusing Navajos. It became a contest to see who could come up with the biggest injustice. Finally, Mr. Toledo gave up."

For a few moments, Spencer let the hum of the air conditioner push conversation from the room. Then, he just had to talk again.

"I still can't see why he feels that way. Benjamin must know some pretty creepy white people."

"I don't think he's given himself the chance to really know any whites," I said.

"What do you mean?"

"It's something my dad told me. If you're looking for something in other people, you usually find it. Everybody's a mixture of bad and good qualities," I said. "If you're looking for the good stuff in people, you find it and the creepy stuff doesn't matter so much. If you never look for the good, you're stuck with the bad."

He nodded slowly, then smiled. "It's like my aunt. She had a fit when Dad told her we were moving to the reservation. She knew exactly what was in store for us: head lice, tuberculosis . . . broken noses from fighting with drunk Indians."

It was my turn to grin.

"She was sure that we were heading for disaster and, when Dad tried to tell her about his visit here, she didn't want to listen."

17

"Have you met Mrs. Blake at the post office?" I asked.
Spence shook his head. "Is she like my aunt?"

"No way, she's a great lady, nice to everybody. But Benjamin doesn't like her."

Spence glanced out the window.

"She's the only one who works at the post office. If she lets me stand at the counter for a minute while she sorts some letters, I don't mind. Benjamin thinks that she lets him wait because he's a Navajo and she's white. He doesn't notice that everybody has to wait once in a while. It makes him mad."

I stood up. We'd been talking too long. Ms. Benally kept looking out at us. In a minute, she'd walk over and ask us if we needed any help with our work. That's her way of reminding students that they ought to be studying, not talking.

"So, that's the way it is," I said. "You'll be happier if you find some good white friends."

"Thanks for the talk, Sam."

It didn't matter that he still had my name mixed up, we wouldn't be seeing that much of one another. I walked to the door. "I guess I'll be seeing you around. Maybe we'll have some classes together or something."

I waited for Spence to follow me, but he just stood there in some kind of deep-thinking trance. It was weird.

Finally, he walked over and slugged me lightly on the arm. "I think you'll see me around all right. I just made up my mind."

"About what?"

"I told you I was an Army brat. I've had lots of practice making friends." He shrugged. "I'm going to make friends with anybody I like, white, brown, green, you name it, even Benjamin and his gang."

I shook my head.

"Don't worry, I won't get you mixed up in my social campaign," Spencer grinned. "But I think you're missing out on a good thing."

"You're crazy!" I said. "I guess you already know that."

He winked. "I'm not sure but I think it's that steady diet of sheep droppings."

Chapter Three

"Sam . . . pssst . . . Sam. . . ."

Through the clatter of after-school locker slamming, I heard the annoying, familiar voice and turned toward it. Spencer West was staring into an almost-empty locker a few doors down.

Without looking in my direction, he spoke from the side of his mouth. "Can I borrow your history notes from the first part of the term? Mrs. Lee said I should get them from somebody because next week's test will cover everything."

He scouted the hallway in both directions, then continued in his loud whisper. "Fake an accident and let them slip to the floor. Leave them there, and I'll pick them up after you walk away. In the morning I'll sneak them into the library and you can get them later. They'll be on the H Shelf in fiction."

I had to laugh. "I feel like a character in some cheap spy movie."

He grinned at me.

I pulled a green notebook from my backpack. "Here. They start right at the front. I already ripped out last term's pages."

"Thanks."

"My notes aren't very good. There's a lot of drawing and stuff. You'll just have to dig out the information."

"Thanks." He flipped through the book, stopping at a sketch of a horse. "This is great!"

I blushed and shrugged.

"Should I use the *H Shelf Plan* to return your notebook?"

"Just give it back to me in class tomorrow. Mrs. Lee may say something important that I'll want to remember."

"You mean just hand it to you . . . like we know each other?" He faked an exaggerated look of astonishment. "Can we talk, too?"

I shot him my *freeze-them-in-their-tracks* stare.

"In case I have questions about your notes. . . ."

My stare continued.

Spencer West held up his hands. "I give up. No questions! No conversation! Not so much as a slight nod of the head in recognition!"

I turned to hide a smile, slammed my locker and headed down the hall toward the front doors.

"Maybe we ought to . . ." he called after me but I didn't stop or turn back. I slipped around the corner and out the front door before he could finish.

After sitting inside all day, the afternoon sunlight was blinding. It felt terrific on my over-airconditioned skin.

Manuelito High is right at a bend in the river and there's only one direction to go when you head home, unless you want to go swimming. Everybody who doesn't ride a bus or have his own car turns east and walks the half mile up the paved road toward what we call "town"—the Texaco station, a trailer park, the post office and Gas and Goodies. I usually turn the opposite direction, to the river, then take the path that wanders back eastwardly alongside the water.

21

It's longer that way but it's quiet. With my sketch pad handy, I'm in no hurry to get home.

As I pushed through the feathery tamarisk into a clear area, a crow's call startled me. He was sitting on the branch of a drifted log at the water's edge on the other side of the river. The log was white and the crow's blackness was such a contrast to the wood and the smooth sand of the bank that I had to get the scene down on paper. I was afraid he'd fly away before I got started but he must have had the same kind of day that I'd had. He just sat there, tired and droopy.

A few quick lines and I had the water, the log, the ridge of sand and sparse grass behind it. Now for the crow. I stared at him, trying to set his image in my mind.

Just as I heard stumbling footsteps and the snapping of tamarisk branches, the crow gave a loud squawk and flew away.

Spencer West, with eyes squinted and hands stretched out in front of him, fumbled his way out of the bushes. He almost stepped on me.

"Watch it!" I said, then added a phrase in Navajo.

"Sorry, I was trying to keep that feathery stuff on those bushes out of my eyes."

"Are you following me?"

Brushing tamarisk wisps from his hair, he looked at my sketch. "What are you doing?"

"Are you following me?"

"Not really." He brushed his shoulders. "Well, maybe I was. . . . Not to spy on you or anything, just to explore the area around here . . . find out what people do after school."

"I'm not *people*. Nobody does what I do so you're checking out the wrong example." I started putting my pad and pencils away.

"Don't let me rush you, Sam. I'll just sit down and wait while you finish drawing that log."

"Before you blundered through the bushes, I was drawing a *crow* sitting on the log."

"Sorry . . . again." He sat down. "Is that why you swore at me in Navajo when I almost stepped on you?"

"I didn't swear at you; I called you a name."

"Same thing, isn't it?"

I began arranging twigs into a design on the sand. "In the first place, there aren't really swear words in Navajo. *Coyote* is as bad as it gets. In the second place, the name I called you was just descriptive: *Walks Like A Bear*."

His face lit up. "You gave me an Indian name?"

"I *called* you a name in Navajo. It wasn't a compliment."

"But, if you thought of a name for me that fits . . ." He looked over at me with that crazy grin. "It's almost like a step toward being friends."

I looked up from the twig design. "Spencer, do you think you're in a Hollywood movie? I guess some tribes are big on giving honorary names, not Navajos. Newborn babies used to be given a war name, but that's not common now. I didn't get one."

"Walks Like A Bear," he said softly. "I like it."

"You're crazy. Bears are sloppy walkers. They don't have to be quiet because they don't have any enemies." I stirred the twigs with my finger, destroying the design. "Of course, you didn't exactly charge through the brush like a bear. I guess the description was all wrong."

Spence laughed. "Maybe that's why I like it. I think I'll hang onto the name. . . . Walks Like A Bear. It's great!"

"Suit yourself. You're the one making a big deal out of this."

I stood up.

He sat there looking up at me.

"I would like you to explain one thing, though." I picked up my backpack and turned to him. "Why me? Out of all the kids sitting in the cafeteria today, out of all the kids in all the classes in school . . . why did you single me out for this treatment?"

"Treatment?"

"Why pick me to be your friend when you don't know me any better than you know anybody else?"

"I have this strategy for making friends. It comes from moving around so much. First, choose someone who seems to have something in common with you. Your tee-shirt was the key." He stood up and started walking along the path and I followed. "I'm not a real Denver Broncos fan but I like sports better than heavy metal rock music and that's what everyone else was advertising on their shirts. I figured I could carry on a halfway interesting conversation about football."

We had to push through another stand of tamarisk, single-file. Spencer waited until we could walk side-by-side again.

"The second strategy is start small. You were eating alone and I thought it might be easier to make friends with one kid than with a group of guys who were already friends. Besides that, you were the only person who wasn't staring at me."

We walked along in silence for a minute, enjoying the sound of the river, the new-green that spring brings to the reservation. Small, bright green leaves on the willows, grass pushing up through the sand, cottonwood and tamarisk and the gray-blue of Russian Olive trees, in most of Carson's Crossing all this freshness would be tired and dusty and wornout in a few weeks. Only here, along the

24

river, would things stay fresh. No wonder I spent a lot of time down here.

Finally, Spencer West cleared his throat.

"What do you do around here for fun?"

"Nothing much," I said. "Those of us who don't have satellite dishes can get two snowy stations on TV and the Boy Scouts show a movie on Friday nights at the elementary school. Usually it's an old Western or a Kung Fu thriller."

"Any sports to play?"

"Some." I shrugged. "There's a tennis court up at the Texaco refinery housing and a softball field and a basketball court. You should talk to Bruce Maxfield about that."

Bruce Maxfield's dad is the plant manager for Texaco. Bruce and his friends would be perfect for a new kid in town.

"I talked to Bruce during Science." Spencer picked up a twisted gray stick and rubbed the sand from it. The wood had been polished by the river. "I was checking out the white kids like you suggested. All Bruce could talk about was his stereo and the new ATV he expects to get for his birthday. He told me about his dad's boat and their camper van. Then he complained about how boring it is to live around here and how dumb the school is and how there isn't anything to do. Bruce Maxfield is the most depressing guy I've ever talked to."

Spencer tapped the stick against the palm of his hand. "I also talked to other white kids. Some of them were nice and some seemed to be jerks. The Navajo kids I talked to were kind of shy, but I found the same thing— a mixture of good guys and jerks.

"The thing is, Sam Nelson, I like to get along with everybody, but I try to get a best friend as soon as I can. A best friend always makes a new place seem like home.

25

"After you took the time to explain Manuelito High society to me, I realized you were my first choice for best friend. Then, I found out you're an honest-to-goodness artist. The clincher was that you laughed at my corny imitation of an undercover spy at the lockers."

He threw the stick into the river and watched it swirl along with the current. "I scared your crow away and you didn't throw me in the river. Instead, you gave me a Navajo name. You must be some kind of a nice guy."

"I *called* you a name."

"Whatever," he went on. "Something has to click when best friends first meet. I felt that click when I talked with you in the lunchroom."

"That was your brain shutting down," I said.

He grinned.

The stick Spencer had thrown floated into a tangle of rocks, brush and wire. The current pushed it upright and it stood for a few seconds, bobbing back and forth. If Spencer West and I became friends, we'd have to be like that stick, standing up to the social current here in Carson's Crossing. Maybe he wanted to waste all that energy, but I sure didn't.

Slowly the stick slid sideways into the water until a ripple grabbed it and pulled it into the mainstream, sweeping it away.

I turned back and started walking. Spencer watched me walk away. In less than a minute he was right beside me again.

The river path runs alongside the wall that circles the Navajo Youth Center. Years ago the center was an old mission. The wall, made from big river rocks, is more than a hundred years old. Spencer stopped and ran his hands over the rocks just as I'd done a thousand times myself.

26

"This whole area looks a little out of place for Carson's Crossing," he said, pulling himself up to sit on top. In the middle of the square made by the rock wall was the center itself, built from the same gray river rocks. Huge cottonwood trees provided shade for the whole place and in that protected area grew lawn, bordered by rabbit brush and wild roses.

I was going to start walking again but it was hot and the shade felt good. After checking to see that no one was around, I pulled myself up on the wall, too.

"I wonder how old these trees are," he said, staring straight up into the giant cottonwoods.

"I don't know. They were probably here when the mission was built."

"This place is a mission?"

"It used to be, a long time ago," I said. "When they were trying to 'civilize' the Navajos. Now, it's a . . . It's not used much."

He turned to inspect the setting behind us. He was right, the youth center was unique. I tried to see it for the first time, the way Spencer West was seeing it. The large main building looked strong, like a castle. The two storage sheds were wooden and needed painting.

I watched Donavan's white cat chase a moth across the lawn. Donavan Walker is one of the VISTA workers who run the youth center. The other worker's name is Josh. If anyone asks him what his last name is, he says, "Call me Josh, just plain Josh." Maybe he has a weird last name. He's a black guy from back East.

VISTA stands for *Volunteers In Service To Americans*. They're like Peace Corps workers, but they have to work with "underprivileged" Americans like us Navajos instead of exotic natives in third world countries. The VISTAS at Carson's Crossing don't seem to mind.

Spence looked over toward the river. "How come they call this place *Carson's Crossing?* Who was Carson?"

"Did you ever hear of Kit Carson?"

"The mountain man? Who hasn't heard of him? You mean he used to cross the river here?"

"He only did it once," I said. "Ever hear of Fort Sumner?"

"I know . . . I know, I missed that question on a history test once." He closed his eyes and recited, "What was the first battle of the Civil War?"

"You missed it again, Einstein. That's Fort Sum*t*er, with a T. This fort, Sumner, was in southern New Mexico. It was a reservation that they pushed the Navajos onto. Because they were starving and had to walk all the way there, hundreds died. Then hundreds more died while they were there because the water was bad and there wasn't enough food, the land wouldn't grow crops. It was a mess.

"Kit Carson was in charge of rounding up the Navajos to take them to Fort Sumner. He burned their crops and orchards and killed most of their livestock. I guess you could say he starved them into surrendering."

"That changes my picture of the grizzly-fighting mountain man," Spencer said.

"One group of Navajos was more stubborn than the others. They came up this way to get away from Carson. He followed them across the river at this point."

"Did he catch them?"

"Nope, they were too tricky. That's why Carson's Crossing has a double meaning around here. Kit Carson crossed the river here but he also got crossed up by fate. He went home empty-handed."

Spence got ready to jump down from the wall.

"Hey," he said, settling down again. "They've got a basketball court here. Do you play?"

28

"Sometimes." I slipped to the ground. Spencer followed me as I walked to the highway and around in front of the old mission. He didn't mention the sign that said, "Navajo Youth Center." Maybe he didn't see it.

Gas and Goodies was about two hundred feet back up the highway on the corner of the school road. I went as far as the store with Spencer and then started to cross to the gas station.

"Do you want to come in?" he asked. "My mom might have some cookies or something."

"Thanks, but I'd better get home."

"Come on, Sam. Just meet my mother and dad," he pleaded. "I don't want them to know I struck out in the social department on my first day at school."

I looked at him.

"Come on . . . cookies . . . homemade chocolate chip cookies."

My empty stomach rumbled. "You know the magic words."

He released a sigh that slid easily into a laugh as he led me around to the back of the store.

Gas and Goodies used to be a trading post so behind the shiny glass and aluminum siding of the new front they added, it was solid, old rock and timber. In the days before pickup trucks, trading posts were important for Navajo survival. They provided food and supplies on the reservation that would normally be found only in town. They also let people buy on credit. Navajos used to rely on their sheep for any money they got. In the spring, they would sell their wool and in the fall they'd sell the extra lambs that had been born earlier in the year. In between the times they had money, the post would let them charge food and clothes, even wood stoves and wagons. Actually, they could get everything they needed at the trading post.

It helped Navajos survive in the middle of nowhere but there was an important disadvantage: people were always in debt. By the time they paid their bill at the trading post with the money from wool, there was nothing left to buy food, so they charged another bill.

Now that most Navajos have some kind of income and modern transportation, trading posts are obsolete. Most people buy in the bigger stores in Farmington, sixty miles away. Even though some older people, like my grandmother, rely on sheep for a living, they haul the wool and sheep to town.

People still remember when the trading post was the center of social life around Carson's Crossing. When they modernized it into Gas and Goodies, they moved the benches from the front and put them under the trees at the side. Just like in the old days, people come in the morning and spend all day sitting around, drinking soda pop and snacking on potato chips. They exchange gossip and reminisce about old times.

The old man that Spencer had tried his new Navajo words on at school was sitting on a bench. He grinned as we walked past. *"Dibe bichaan bith thlikaan,"* he said, chuckling.

Spencer's face turned red, as he laughed and shrugged.

Mrs. West didn't have any cookies but she let us have a package of Twinkies and a glass of milk. After Spencer introduced me as Sam Nelson, I couldn't think of any way to straighten out the mixup.

When she brought the milk into the store from the housing in back, she told us that Mr. West had gone into town for some merchandise after registering Spence at school. He wasn't back yet.

"Your father said you couldn't take German."

Spence swallowed. "No. The only language class they offer is Beginning Spanish but I decided to take an art class instead of a foreign language. I'll work at picking up Navajo on my own."

His mother turned her attention to me.

"I'm so glad Spencer found a friend today," she said. "It's hard to start in a new school at the end of the year."

"He gave me a Navajo name, 'Walks Like A Bear,' " Spencer said.

Mrs. West beamed at me and I winced. I was wolfing down her Twinkies; how could I tell her that her son and I weren't really friends?

"Where do you live, Sam?" Mrs. West asked as she cleaned the glass on their milk case. She called me Sam, too. That killed me. Maybe I'd have to change my name.

"I live in a trailer across the highway, over behind the gas station," I said.

"Do you have brothers and sisters?"

"I have five." I watched her stagger, leaving fingerprints on the clean glass as she steadied herself.

"Oh," she said, recovering. "Spencer has a younger brother, David. He's in fourth grade."

"My little brother Anson is in fourth grade."

"Six people live in a trailer?" Spence asked.

"It was eight for a long time, counting my mom and dad," I said. "This year my sister, Adelia, is away at college and Russell will be going into the Marines in a couple of months, after he graduates. We have another house out at Red Rock by my grandmother's and we have a hogan at the sheep camp but, during the school year,

31

we all live here in town so we can go to the games and stuff.''

"It must be pretty crowded over there," Mrs. West said.

"A little, but we're used to it. Sometimes the younger kids ride the school bus to Red Rock and stay with my grandmother or my Aunt Irene. For Navajos, aunts and uncles are like mothers and fathers, and cousins are brothers and sisters. It's like one big family. Everybody looks after everybody else.''

"I guess that would make up for the crowded conditions," Spence said.

"I guess." I wasn't sure that family support was an even trade for a room of my own.

"I'd better be going. Thanks a lot for the Twinkies and milk. I'll see you later, *Walks Like A Bear*," I said with a smirk.

He followed me out the door. "Do you have work to do at home?"

I hesitated. Then, I thought about the Twinkies and glass of milk. "I'm going to play basketball over at the youth center.''

"Where?"

"At the Navajo Youth Center, the old mission we stopped at on the way home.''

His eyes lit up. "Do you think it'd be all right if I came along?"

"I can't stop you from showing up over there, but what I said in the library still goes. Benjamin and Freeman and the other guys will be there and there won't be any white kids. Anglos play up at Texaco.''

"I'll take my chances."

"It's your funeral, Spencer West." I turned to go. "You're on your own. I'm going home to change my clothes and then I'll head over to the center. It's better for both of us if we don't go together.''

He just looked at me.

''Maybe you'll find somebody else in a football tee-shirt, a better prospect to become your best friend.''

He didn't joke or contradict me, just shrugged his shoulders.

Chapter Four

Johnny and Alex were practicing foul shots with some kids from the elementary school while everybody else lounged around on the lawn. Little kids weren't asked to play in actual games but they hung around anyway. I guess they knew they'd get their chance to take over the youth center. When kids my age started making the high school varsity sports teams, we'd consider the center "minor league" and stop playing there, just like the guys before us had done.

Donavan stood, leaning against one of the big trees. Benjamin sat next to the same tree, using it as a backrest. Donavan blew softly on the metal whistle in his mouth, a habit he has when we're sitting around waiting for a game to get started.

He let the whistle drop and it slid to the end of the leather thong circling his neck. "*Ya'at'eeh*, Nelson," he said. He uses the little Navajo he knows whenever he can.

"Hi," I said. None of the others said anything. They weren't ignoring me, that's just their way.

"How's it going?" Donavan asked. "Any excitement at your end of town?"

That's his usual joke. He knows that in a place as small

as Carson's Crossing, there is no *end of town;* the end of town is also the center of town.

Benjamin sat up like he might like to join the conversation but Josh called to us. "You gentlemen going to play a little basketball today, or spend the time resting up for supper?"

Josh couldn't stand to see us just sitting there. He didn't play basketball himself but he was always busy. If he wasn't working on the center's old pickup, like now, he was fixing up one of the wooden buildings or gardening.

For once, I was glad he was pushing us into a game. Maybe it would be easier for Spencer to join in when everyone was warming up instead of sitting around.

Players were still moving toward the cracked concrete court when attention shifted to the lanky white kid coming through the gate in baggy gym shorts and droopy socks.

"Hi," Spence said. "I was just passing by and thought I'd see what kind of basketball you guys play."

His smile was brave but he kept wiping the palms of his hands against his thighs.

It took Donavan and Josh a couple of minutes to introduce themselves and find out a few things about the West family.

Then, Benjamin walked over. "Hello, you old goat," he said in Navajo and everybody laughed, even Spencer.

Spence said, "I hope you can come home with me for some of my favorite food one of these days."

It took a few seconds for it to sink in but Benjamin finally got the joke and looked over at me suspiciously. I studied the cement.

"Did you see the sign on the gate, *Bilagaana?*" Benjamin asked. "It says *Navajo* Youth Center."

"Hey, what kind of a . . ." Donavan began, but Spencer interrupted him.

35

"I saw the sign. It says Navajo *Youth* Center. You're Navajo. I'm a youth."

Benjamin just looked at him.

Donavan's whistle split the silence. "Come on, men, let's get going. Five minutes for warm-up drills."

"Do you want to spend all day debating the meaning of that sign out front or are you going to teach me some basketball?" Spencer West asked.

"I don't think you can teach a crazy white man anything," one of the boys said in Navajo.

"They're not too smart," Benjamin said. "But I think we can share a few tips with him . . . like, *Stay away from places where you aren't welcome.*"

One of the things I liked best about the youth center was that we were on our own most of the time. Josh kept working on the pickup, an antique Ford donated to the center by the Texaco plant so that we could learn auto mechanics. Donavan watched the warm-up drills, blew his whistle one more time and told us to choose up teams, then went inside to work with some girls on stringing the loom he'd finished building the week before. He planned to help all of us keep in touch with our traditional arts and crafts. There was one problem with that idea—the only thing we boys really wanted to do was play basketball, so a few girls and the two VISTA workers themselves were the only ones benefiting from the enrichment programs.

Actually, I wouldn't have minded a little refereeing for this particular game, but I couldn't think of a way to sneak over and ask Josh without drawing attention to myself. If things got too hot, I hoped he'd notice and cool them off.

We went through the ritual of choosing up sides, a waste of time because the teams were always the same. Spencer ended up a *skin* with me, no surprise. When we

36

took off our shirts, I whispered, "Be careful, these guys play rough."

"Thanks, I'll watch myself," he whispered back.

You'd be better off watching the other guys, I thought.

For the first few minutes, nobody passed the ball to Spencer. They stepped in front of him, tried to trip him, stopped short so he'd run into them, but he managed to stay out of trouble. Whenever I got the ball, he'd call, "Sam, over here!" But somebody would cover him before I could pass.

Finally, Benjamin got the ball and stopped playing. He stood absolutely still, the ball cradled between his arm and his chest. He waited for everyone's attention. It didn't take long.

"Hey, Gas and Goodies boy," he said, "why do you keep calling Nelson by his last name?"

Spencer looked over at me in confusion.

Alex chimed in, "Don't you understand English, man?"

"If you're going to keep shouting at Nelson, at least call him by his first name." Benjamin spat on the court.

Spencer West looked over at me again, then back to Benjamin.

"The whole thing's my fault," I said. "When I told him my name, he got it mixed up and I haven't set it straight. It's no big deal. It doesn't bother me."

"It bothers me," Benjamin said, looking for a fight.

"What are you guys talking about?" Spencer asked, looking from face to face.

"This is Nelson Sam," Benjamin said, pointing to me. "His name is Nelson, you dumb *Bilagaana*."

Spencer started to smile as the light dawned. "You mean your name is Nelson Sam?" He started to laugh.

"What's so funny about that?" Benjamin said but Spencer ignored him.

"Your name is Nelson and you let me call you Sam all day?"

Benjamin and the others just looked at each other. I couldn't help it, I had to grin.

Spence was really laughing now. "I . . . I introduced you to my mom . . . as . . . Sam Nelson."

We both stood there and laughed even though it wasn't that funny. Some of the others joined in just because we were laughing.

"Why didn't you tell me I had it backwards, you dope?"

Benjamin's temper flared again. "Who are you calling a *dope,* stupid *Bilagaana?*"

Again, Spence ignored him. "Mom told my dad all about Spence's new friend, Sam Nelson." A new attack of laughter. "Right this minute, she's probably writing to my Aunt Rebecca about you and your five brothers and sisters, the Nelson family."

More crazy laughter while Benjamin and his friends watched us in disgust and exchanged puzzled glances.

By the time we finished laughing, I knew I was doomed to have Spencer West for a friend. Somehow we'd work it out so we could stay out of trouble.

"Let's just play," Benjamin said, "and leave this *Bilagaana* laughing at his own joke."

Spence coughed. "I'm ready, *kl'izi sani.*" He laid his hand on Benjamin's shoulder. "Let's play."

Benjamin shrugged his hand away. "Don't call me that."

"No offense. Somebody told me it was a title of great respect."

A couple of kids laughed but Benjamin just turned his back and stomped to the other side of the court.

The game started again. Spence stole the ball from Freeman and got the chance to show us what he could do, which was pretty impressive. Although I saw Benjamin's eyes open wide in surprise a couple of times, his scowl did a good job of hiding any respect for Spence's skill with a basketball.

The players on the skins team started loosening up a little and passing the ball to Spencer. This was the first time that we'd ever had a chance to beat Benjamin's team and there was no denying that our advantage was Spencer West. The shirts tried every trick they could think of but we edged ahead to take the win. We were so excited that everyone was clapping one another on the back.

Slowly, the skins became aware of Benjamin watching them and started backing away. Still, they couldn't hide a hint of appreciation, of warmth, in their eyes as they glanced over at Spencer.

I thought maybe basketball would be the way for Spence and Benjamin to become friends. Maybe they had something in common after all. But, as we pulled shirts down over our sticky backs, Benjamin spoke up.

"Hey, *Bilagaana!* Since your dad's running that fancy store, maybe we can all come over for some free pop."

Spence shook his head. "Not today, I'm afraid. I'd like to be able to treat you guys, but right now I'm not sure how good business is going to be. Maybe next month."

"I just thought you wanted to be friends, white man," Benjamin sneered.

"I do want to be your friend, all of you. But I don't want to buy your friendship."

"Forget it, *Bilagaana,*" Benjamin said. "We wouldn't drink white man's pop anyway."

Spence just grinned. "What other kind of pop is there, besides white man's pop?"

Benjamin didn't answer.

"See you guys later," I said. I've got to get home."

I started across the court and noticed Spence following me. I broke into a run and left him behind.

As I went through the youth center gate I heard Benjamin shouting something in Navajo. I think he said, "White dogs should run with their own kind."

Up the road I slowed down and let Spencer West catch up.

"For a minute there, I thought we were going to be friends," he said.

"We are, but there's no need to advertise it."

He gave me a puzzled look. "You mean we're friends but it's a secret?"

"Not a secret exactly, we just have to work things out so that we avoid trouble."

A funny grin slid onto his face. "I don't think friendship works like that, but I like you, so we'll try it your way."

He slugged me lightly on the shoulder. "Just make sure you let me know your terrific plan for avoiding trouble as soon as you make one up . . . friend."

Chapter Five

When I got home, everything was quiet, a rare occasion at our trailer. Usually the tan aluminum siding is quivering from the chaos inside. Today it seemed out of place to slam the door, so I closed it slowly, pulling until the latch caught. Then I went through the living room to the kitchen door and paused.

My mother was sitting at the table working on a jigsaw puzzle. She loves those things. It used to be a problem finding space in the trailer to set one up, then Dad made her a puzzle board. He put a raised border around the edge with strips of wood so the pieces don't slip off. When she puts it away, a smaller board fits right inside the rim to hold the puzzle flat. Hooks on each side hold the boards together so Mom can stand the puzzle against the wall, out of the way. My dad's pretty smart when it comes to inventing things.

Mom picked up a puzzle piece, tried it, put it back and kept looking. She was concentrating so hard she didn't notice me. I watched her for a minute, admiring her patience, enjoying how the evening sun slid through the window onto her hair. It was smoothed back into a traditional Navajo double-bun, tied with strands of white yarn.

My mother is a mixture of modern and traditional. Her hair, the heavy, turquoise-and-silver jewelry she wears all the time, her quickness to speak Navajo rather than English make her seem kind of old-fashioned. But those traditional parts of her blend well with her more modern clothes, slacks and tennis shoes, and rose-tinted glasses with shiny frames.

She found a piece that fit and pressed it into place with a tiny snap.

"Where is everybody?" I asked, walking over to inventory the refrigerator.

She looked up quickly. "*Yai!* You scared me, *shiyazh.* Don't sneak up behind people that way."

"It's an old Indian trick."

"Be careful or you won't live to be an old Indian," she teased and I laughed.

In Navajo, she told me that Russell was running, as usual. Yvonne was using the phone at the station to talk with her girlfriend, Lucille. Anson had conned Dad out of a pop for himself and his new friend and they'd gone over to the elementary school playground. And Rosemary was playing Barbies with her friends at the trailer court.

"The potatoes are frying on low heat and the dough is shaped to pat into tortillas," she said, putting the puzzle board together. "I'm going to do that now; will you set the table?"

"You want me to do women's work?" I said in mock surprise, knowing the answer already.

"Do you want to eat?"

When I finished, I went to my room to think about how to be friends with Spencer West without drawing the attention of the whole reservation. My mother's jigsaw puzzle stayed on my mind.

I don't help her with one very often because it's frustrating. I end up wishing I had a hammer to *make* the pieces fit. But, once in a while when I have nothing else to do, I'll sit down for a few minutes of torture at the puzzle board. A couple of times I've had the strange experience of one piece almost jumping up and down, shouting, "Here I am! I'm the one you're looking for!" When I move that piece over to the puzzle, it slides right into place as though the matching pieces are pulling it out of my hand.

That was the way the friendship developed between me and Spencer West. I guess it's the *click* Spence was talking about. For me, it happened at the basketball game. When we finished laughing about my mixed up name, I felt as though we'd been friends all our lives.

The trouble with puzzles, jigsaw *and* the friendship kind, is that once one problem is solved, there are still hundreds of others to work out. I promised Spence a plan that would let us avoid problems and still be friends but all I could think up was the secret friend idea. For the next few weeks, we hung around together at one another's homes and down at the river but at school and the youth center, public places, we were just two loners joining in with the group, carefully arriving and leaving separately.

Spence told me he thought it took more energy to avoid trouble than facing it straight on.

"I can't explain it, Spence. It's just the way I am—a shadowman."

"All this sneaking around is kind of silly but, if you think it's working out, I'll go along with you, Sam Nelson. . . . I mean Nelson Sam," he said with a grin.

The truth was, I didn't feel it was working out. I'd blended into the scenery all my life but I'd never been a phony before and it gave me a bad feeling. At the same time, whenever I thought about coming out of the shadows into the spotlight with Benjamin and his friends in the audience, I didn't feel so good either.

At school, Spence was relaxed and friendly with every student, Navajos and whites. And he still showed up almost daily at the youth center—playing ball, sliding his way into conversations, saying funny things even though the laughter didn't last long most of the time. I was hoping that someday soon the Benjamin bunch would accept him as part of the group. I just kept waiting.

One Saturday morning in April, Mom sent me to the store for a gallon of milk.

"Are we still meeting at the center to help Josh with the truck?" Spence gave me my change.

"I guess so. You're the one who wants to spend a Saturday afternoon leaning over a rusty fender, skinning his knuckles, working grease under his fingernails. . . ."

"I can hardly wait for the fun to start!"

"That kind of fun I can get at the station with my dad. But Josh's mechanics program could really use a boost, so I'm going over right after lunch."

"See you there, Shadowman," he teased.

As I reached the benches under the trees, a big orange-and-white recreational vehicle pulled up. Before the dust had even settled, a chubby, bald man wearing Bermuda shorts, sandals, and a bright yellow tee-shirt with red lettering, "I Love Colorado," climbed down from the driver's seat and walked around to the side door.

"Come on, Myra," the man called as he opened the door. "Every time we stop, you comb your hair and put on lipstick. If you think you're going to bump into Robert Redford at a dump like this, think again. Now, move it!"

I couldn't resist seeing Myra in her fresh lipstick so I

44

sat down. As the man turned toward the trading post, he saw me.

"Oh, hello," he said, raising his hand like they do in old westerns on TV. I was glad he didn't say, "How."

I nodded to him.

"You have much land around here," the man said, spreading his arms out. As his blond wife climbed down and walked over to us, he asked, "Do you get much rain?" He pointed to the sky and then to the ground. "You know, sky water."

It was kind of funny, but annoying, too. If these people had been through Colorado, they should have learned that real Indians aren't much like the feathered idiots you see in movies. The woman glanced from my solemn face to her husband's and back again, finally releasing a nervous giggle.

"It rains occasionally this time of year," I said, thinking of the longest words I could. "But generally, we receive substantial precipitation in August or the later parts of autumn."

The woman giggled again and poked her husband with her elbow. "You and your *sky water*, Felix. This young man speaks American!"

Turning back to me, she said, "Talk a little Indian for us."

I forced a stern expression to freeze across my face. The woman was lumping all Indians together. She should have asked me to speak some *Navajo* because each tribe is different from other tribes. Apaches speak Apache and Sioux speak Sioux, but to her I guess all Indians talk *Indian*.

The woman pulsed with excitement, melting my resentment. Give her a thrill, I thought.

45

"Kl'izi choon ayoo da nith choon," I said. Billy goats smell terrible.

Just as I was *talking Indian,* Spence walked up. He'd learned some Navajo in the short time he'd been here. I helped him every day and some of the people who came into the store gave him words and phrases. He made plenty of mistakes but his enthusiasm was so infectious that everyone wanted to help him that much more.

As he stood there listening, his look of concentration slid into a grin.

Myra giggled. "What did you say?"

"I said that you bring special beauty to our empty land."

She blushed, her hands flying up to clap against her cheeks.

Felix said, "Well, I'll be . . ." He patted me on the back. "Let me buy you a soda for those beautiful words of friendship."

While Felix went in to get me a Coke, I introduced Myra to Spence. As soon as her husband came back, she made him turn right around and buy a Coke for Spence, too. We sat around with them for half-an-hour and they asked all sorts of dumb questions about Indian agents and buffalo hunting. Gradually, a little light began to break through the fog in their empty heads. They started to understand the way things really are on *Indian land,* as Felix called the reservation.

Finally, they asked about camping places. I told them about a spot right on the river not far from the youth center with a few trees and a circle of rocks for a campfire. I gave them directions but, before they drove off to *really rough it,* Felix's words again, they insisted on buying us candy bars.

*   *   *

Three hours of handing Josh wrenches was all the boost we could muster for his mechanics program. We came home the private way, along the river.

Felix was at the camping place we'd recommended, roasting hot dogs over an open fire.

"He's probably wishing he had buffalo meat on that stick," Spence said.

All of a sudden, I really wanted to pump a little excitement into their trip. After coming all this way, they should go home with a real Indian country adventure to tell their neighbors.

"You're crazy," Spence said, when I explained my plan.

"Come on, it won't hurt anybody. Felix and Myra will have fun. We'll have fun."

"Somebody might have a heart attack."

"No way! This just might turn out to be the highlight of their whole trip."

Finally, Spence agreed.

"If something goes wrong, you do all the explaining," he said.

I just laughed. "Meet me at the big tree, upstream from the campground, and bring David."

"David?" He groaned. "That's all I need, the family snitch!"

"We need all the man power we can get. I'll bring Anson and the stuff we need. Don't forget to wear your swimming trunks under your clothes."

That night, by the time my little brother and I had stumbled through the dark to the tree, Spence and David were already in their swimming suits.

"I brought the supplies," I said, dropping the box to the sand.

"Now, what?" Spence asked.

"Now we go over to the river and rub mud all over ourselves."

"We what?"

I started for the riverbank. "Come on, warriors. It's a little trick I learned from watching movies. We have to camouflage you white men. This party is just for Indians."

"Don't be shy, Walks Like A Bear." Anson laughed.

Spence had told everyone about his Navajo name. In a way, Anson was teasing him but, like Spence, he considered it a compliment.

I scooped up some mud and started smearing it on my legs. Anson took a handful and held it for a few seconds. "Nelson, we *are* Indians. We don't need to be any darker."

"Do you want Spence and David to have all the fun?"

"And all the pneumonia?" Spence added, gasping as he rubbed mud across his chest.

I'd forgotten how cold the night wind can be in the spring. As we stood there shivering, I started to doubt the brilliance of my plan but I didn't want to admit it.

Taking orange and yellow poster paint from the box, I painted lines and circles on the others: their faces, chests, even their arms. Then Spence painted me. We tied strips of cloth around our heads and stuck some spiny yucca leaves in our headbands for feathers. Then I wrapped other strips of cloth around some sticks and dipped them into our kerosene can. We were ready.

"Now, listen, men," I whispered. "When we get close enough, I'll light the torches and then we really have to make a lot of noise. If we aren't loud enough, they might sleep right through our show and have nothing to tell their friends back home. Just yell and jump and whoop it up, like Indians in old movies do."

48

We crept up the hill until we were about twenty feet from the RV. It was dark except for one light.

It had to be dark for the surprise to work so we waited. The seconds crept by and I was just about to call the whole thing off when the light went out.

After counting slowly to ten, I lit the torches. One mighty coyote call and we attacked! We ran around the RV, shouting and yipping, sending ear-splitting war whoops into the night sky. We threw our torches up in the air, picked them up after they hit the ground, then threw them again. We deserved an Oscar for The-Most-Enthusiastic-Performance-Staged-In-The-Open-By-Freezing-Actors.

Every once in a while, we could hear Myra telling Felix, "Do something, for crying out loud!"

Finally Felix shouted, "What do you want me to do, honey? Call the Cavalry?"

We whooped and danced for a couple of minutes until the torches burned out. Then we staggered through the dark back to the river, satisfied that we'd done our best to give the tourists a little excitement. We might have been too enthusiastic because, as we reached the bank, we heard the RV start up and saw its lights as it backed around and headed out to the road.

Then we whooped and laughed some more. The only bad part was washing the mud and paint off. We had to get it all off or answer questions when we got home. I was glad Anson and I had begun sleeping in the back of the pickup now that spring was here. It isn't easy to sneak into a trailer at midnight.

The water in the river seemed even colder than before as we rinsed off the mud and paint. Finally, I took a deep breath, jumped right in and scrubbed myself as fast as I could. When I came out, there was still paint on my chest so I went in again. Pretty soon the others joined me and we hollered some more at the shock of the cold water.

Then we got out, took off our wet trunks, struggled into our other clothes and started for home. There was a distinct possibility that we'd all get sick but it was worth the risk if we'd made the visit more memorable for our good friends, Felix and Myra.

Anson and I walked Spence and David back to Gas and Goodies. We weren't worried about their safety but we wanted to settle down from the excitement of our adventure. The two younger kids were scuffling around behind Spence and me, trying to trip one another. We came up on the store from behind and, when we rounded the corner of the building and stopped suddenly, they ran into us.

"Watch it, you jerk," Anson said. Then he looked up and saw why we'd put on the brakes so fast.

The orange and white RV was parked in front of the store, and Felix was pacing alongside it. He glanced over, saw us standing there, and leaped toward his vehicle. Unfortunately, Myra stepped out the side door at the same moment and they ran into each other. As they bounced apart, Felix looked over again. Finally, he recognized us.

"Oh, hello, kids," he said with an embarrassed glance at the ground. "I thought you might be some of those renegades."

"Renegades?" Spence asked and his voice squeaked.

"There's a whole tribe of . . ." He stopped as the door to Gas and Goodies opened.

"They'll send someone around as soon as the new shift starts," Mr. West said. "How many did you say there were?"

"At least a dozen," Felix said.

"Closer to twenty, honey." Myra glanced nervously over her shoulder.

"I've got to be honest with you folks, the Navajo Police dispatcher sounded skeptical. I think they're going to take their time sending an officer out this far . . . if they send someone at all."

"Out this far?" Now Felix looked over his shoulder.

Spence's dad explained. "The headquarters is almost fifty miles away. The dispatcher, Mrs. Tso, said they used to have a policeman stationed here but right now their man power is low and it's usually pretty quiet around Carson's Crossing so they've closed the area."

"Just my luck," Felix said glumly.

Mrs. West came out with two cups of coffee and handed them to the Indian uprising victims. She and Mr. West noticed us at the same time.

"Where have you boys been?" she asked.

There was an uncomfortable silence and then we spoke in unison.

"At the high school."

"Over to Anson's."

"The school playground."

"Hanging around the youth center."

After another uncomfortable silence, Spence said, "We've been sort of traveling around the neighborhood."

"So it seems," his father said and studied us carefully.

Myra broke the tension when she shivered. "It was terrible. I'll never forget those blood-curdling screams."

Spence's dad was still looking at us. Then he turned to Felix and Myra. "Why don't you folks just pull your vehicle around in back. It's all fenced and I guarantee you'll be safe for the night. Try and get a good night's rest and resume your trip refreshed in the morning."

"I don't know," Felix said.

"The boys will help me stand guard if it will make you feel better."

51

We looked at one another.

"Let's try it," Myra said, handing her untouched cup back to Mrs. West. "I'm beginning to unwind a little and we wouldn't be a mile down the road before you'd be asleep at the wheel."

With a sigh, Felix nodded and handed over his cup.

"I'll open the gate." Mrs. West set the coffee by the door and started off around the building. Myra followed her and Felix climbed into the RV.

We watched the big van roll around to the gate.

"I guess I'll see you tomorrow," I said, walking away.

"Don't forget your box," Mr. West said and nodded toward our container of renegade supplies. I'd set it down behind us, out of sight, and forgotten it. Then, like a dope, I walked away, leaving all that incriminating evidence in the bright glow of Gas and Goodies' floodlights.

"Thanks. I almost forgot . . ." I glanced at Spence, "my school project."

Spence's father grinned.

"Dad, we probably ought to tell you . . ." Spence began.

"I don't want to know."

"But . . ."

"I really don't want to hear about it tonight, son."

He walked over to David and rubbed his ear lobe, then held his hand in the light so we could see the orange paint.

"School project," he said and snorted a laugh.

We looked at one another again.

"No harm done," Mr. West went on. "As a matter of fact, it seems to me that someone went to a lot of trouble to show a pretty exciting time to a couple of tourists."

He laid a hand on each of his son's shoulders. "That man's story just keeps growing. By morning, it will rival the Battle of Little Bighorn."

We sighed in relief.

"No, sir," he said to himself. "I don't want to hear any more about it tonight." He laid one arm over Spence's shoulder and the other over David's and started walking them into the store. "Of course, that doesn't mean that I won't want the complete story in a day or two."

Anson and I headed for home.

Dad was waiting for us, sitting on the tailgate of the pickup.

"Give you a hand?" he asked, standing to take the box from me and studying its contents before he set it on the ground next to the trailer steps.

"I thought so," he said.

Anson and I looked at one another in the moonlight.

"Sylvia Tso called from the Navajo Police to see if I'd had any drunks hanging around the station . . . any fellows who might want to harrass some tourists. I told her that things were pretty calm around here but I'd keep my eyes open."

We looked at the ground now instead of each other.

"I was working late or I'd have missed the call."

"Dad . . ."

"I got a little worried and decided it was time to go home so I could check on you two sleeping out here." He sat down on the tailgate again. "You weren't here and I started getting a little more worried."

"Dad, it was kind of a joke."

He waited.

"Anson was there, too," I said defensively.

"Whose idea was it?"

I studied the rust on the side of the truck.

"I thought so," Dad said.

"We just wanted to give those tourists something to remember about Carson's Crossing."

"A heart attack?" I thought I could see a slight smile.

"I really like those two."

I decided to start at the beginning. "At first, I thought Felix and Myra were kind of dumb, thinking that real Indians were like movie Indians. But after Spence and I talked with them for a little while, they seemed to catch on to how things are around here."

My father put his hand on my shoulder as I sat down next to him. Anson climbed into the pickup bed and curled up on his sleeping bag.

"I'm confused, son," Dad said. "You wanted those visitors to get a true picture of you, of Navajos, and the reservation. You spent time helping them understand. Then you pull a stunt right out of Hollywood, something to put your new friends back on the wrong track."

I shivered. Was it the wind, the river's chill still running through me? . . . Or his words?

"I didn't think of it that way. . . . I just wanted to do something for them . . . something they'd think was really great." Dad patted my back and I went on. "I guess I goofed it up pretty bad, huh?"

"I think so."

He stood up and the tailgate rose with a squeak. "You gave them a memorable experience and I think they'll appreciate it even more when they know why you did it and all the trouble you went to for them."

"How will they know?"

He turned and looked at me.

"I guess I could go over and explain in the morning."

Dad continued to look at me.

"I'll talk to them first thing in the morning."

"Good night," Dad said and went in, leaving the box next to the steps.

But it wasn't a good night. I spent the first half of it rehearsing how I'd explain everything to Felix and Myra, and the rest of it worrying about how they'd accept my explanation.

First thing in the morning I hurried over to talk to them before I lost my nerve, but they were already gone. I felt bad about the whole thing: the misinformation, their big scare, the stories they'd tell at home. I vowed never to be so stupid again.

Chapter Six

The following week in English class, Mrs. Bolton decided to give us one of her composition fluency drills. We choose our own topic and write for five minutes without stopping. For some kids, five minutes seems like five hours. I don't mind the assignment because she doesn't correct our spelling or check capital letters and commas. "The purpose of the writing is to start your ideas flowing and record those ideas," she always says.

The room was getting quiet and my ideas were ready to flow. There was just one problem, no pencil. I don't know what happened to it but the one I slid into my back pocket before lunch was gone.

When Mrs. Bolton is ready to start the timer, anyone who doesn't have a sharpened pencil and paper in hand, has to sweat in the spotlight while the whole class listens to the lecture—"Being prepared in class is the first step to being prepared in life."

"Dolores, do you have an extra pencil?" I called softly.

She shook her head with a sympathetic glance.

"Nelson," somebody whispered and I turned around. Benjamin Nez was offering me a ballpoint pen.

"Thanks."

He shrugged.

I wrote about Felix and Myra, changing the details so it sounded like I made it up. Mrs. Bolton wouldn't have believed I'd do such a strange thing anyway.

After class, I gave the pen back to Benjamin and we walked down the hall together.

"I can't stand that guy," Benjamin said, pointing down the hall ahead of us with his lips, the Navajo way.

"Who?"

"That white kid, his majesty Spencer West."

My heart started beating faster. "How come you don't like him. . . . He seems pretty friendly."

"That's just an act. He's like all the other pushy *Bila-gaanas*." He reached out, tapped somebody on the shoulder and turned away so that when the victim looked around, he couldn't tell who'd tapped him. "Freeman told me that he's even given himself a Navajo name, *Roars Like A Bear*."

"Not *Roars*. . . ." I stopped myself just in time.

"I know. It doesn't even fit him."

I stopped at the drinking fountain, thinking he'd go on to his next class, but he waited for me.

I could have said, "That's no act; Spence really does like other people." I wanted to say, "He's a good person; give yourself a chance to get to know him." Things I *should* say bounced around in my mind, but my pounding heart kept them from coming out my mouth. Walking alongside Benjamin Nez, listening to him put down my friend, I was miserable. But I was even more miserable because I didn't stand up for Spence.

"He pushed his way into the youth center, didn't he?"

"I think he just likes to play basketball."

"Well, he ought to play over at Texaco with his own kind."

"It's two miles up to the plant."

"That's his problem."

"You know how lazy whites can be when it comes to walking," I said, wondering how I could say such a rotten thing. At the same time, I found myself searching for even more rotten things to patronize Benjamin.

I didn't say anything while we maneuvered around the group of cheerleader hopefuls practicing for tryouts.

Then I came to my senses a little and tried to think of something to help Benjamin get to know Spence better. It came out almost as cowardly as the other had. "You know how terrible the Texaco team is. That West kid is a good player; maybe he wants to play with us because we're good."

"Some of us are." Benjamin punched me playfully on the arm and laughed, an encouraging sign.

Then, he laid his arm across my shoulders. "You really ought to talk to your little brother, Nelson."

"My little brother?"

"The one in grade school. He's running around with West's little brother all the time."

He leaned closer and spoke coldly into my ear. "It isn't a good thing."

"They're just kids." I tried to laugh, to lighten the weight of his arm across my back. "What do little kids know?"

"Nothing. Kids don't know nothing unless you teach them." Benjamin let his arm slide off my shoulder. "That's why you need to talk to him, explain things to him."

"Maybe I will," I said, slowing down so that he would move on.

The tight feeling in my stomach, shame for being such a coward, stayed with me a long time.

*   *   *

When I walked through the gate at the youth center late that afternoon, Benjamin was playing Horse with Freeman and Alex. Spence was leaning over the old Ford's engine with Josh. Donavan was sitting on the grass at the edge of the basketball court watching the Horse players.

In Horse, the players start out with four imaginary horses and take turns trying to make baskets from different positions on the court. If the player before you makes a basket, you have to make the same kind of shot from the same position. If you miss, you lose a horse. When you miss four shots, you're out of the game. Alex was down to one horse because his turn came after Benjamin's and Benjamin has this very tricky jump shot from the far right side. As soon as Alex was out of the game, Benjamin would go to work on Freeman, using the same shot. He always wins that way.

I sat down next to Donavan.

"Ya' at' eeh, sik' is," he said. Hello, my friend.

"Ya' at' eeh."

"Are you ready for a red hot basketball game?"

"Are you going to ref?"

"Somebody has to," he said. "Ever since Spence showed up, you guys have been playing for blood."

"Not all of us." I watched Benjamin finish off Freeman with a flick of his wrist and a big grin.

The three went inside to get a drink.

A few minutes later some other boys came in the gate and stood around on the court talking.

Dribbling the basketball down the sidewalk, Benjamin spoke in Navajo. "Let's get playing."

Spence looked over, then started toward the court.

"Not you, white ape," Benjamin called to him in Navajo and the others laughed. "At your very best you play

59

like a three-year-old; today, with car grease on your hands, you'll never hold onto the ball.''

"What did he say?'' Donavan asked.

I shrugged. "Something about greasy hands from working on the pickup.''

"Benjamin doesn't like Spencer much, does he?''

I shrugged again.

"It's too bad. They're both good guys.''

When we were choosing up sides, I was surprised when Benjamin made Spence his first choice. After a few minutes of play, I understood Benjamin's strategy. Nobody on his team was passing the ball to Spence. Time after time, when Spence was wide open, Benjamin passed up scoring opportunities by giving the ball to someone in a poorer position.

Spence fouled me, trying to steal the ball. Donavan called a time-out and Spence went in to the drinking fountain.

As the rest of us slowly started into position for the foul shot, a dusty car stopped at the gate. Two young men climbed out, stretched for a few seconds and started toward us. Donavan walked over to meet them.

"Hello,'' the driver, a blond with flushed cheeks, said. Then he started making sounds that made no sense at all.

The other dark-haired man just nodded and smiled.

We all joined Donavan and watched him try to figure out what was going on.

The blond finally shook his head, then spoke slowly. "I . . . do . . . not . . . speak English,'' he said with a strange accent.

Donavan gave a friendly laugh and, very slowly, he said, "I do not speak anything else.''

The two men responded with more talking and puzzled expressions.

Spence came up behind the group just then and let loose a long string of sounds. The strangers' faces lit up and they both started talking to Spence. More than a few eyes opened wide as Spence kept answering them. There were lots of pauses on Spence's side of the conversation and plenty of "uh"s as he stalled for time, but still the strange sounds flew back and forth.

Spence turned to Donavan. "These guys are from Germany. They're touring the whole country."

The dark man said something.

Spence laughed. "They were hoping to see some Indians."

"Well, here we are," I said.

One of the men spoke again, Spence responded, then the other man said something. The pattern repeated a few times.

"What are they saying?" Benjamin asked.

"They just have some questions about the reservation and Navajos."

"What are you telling them?" Benjamin glared.

Spence grinned. "Nothing bad, Benjamin, my man."

The group didn't seem assured. Their gaze jumped from speaker to speaker like the audience in a tennis match.

Donavan was watching our faces. "Spence talking with these visitors in German is kind of like you guys talking Navajo around him, isn't it? It makes you uneasy." He grinned. "I wonder if Spence feels that way when he knows you're talking about him but doesn't understand what you're saying."

Some of the boys looked at one another, a few looked at their feet. Benjamin's smoldering look said, So what?

Spence was talking and pointing down the road. "Does Cedar Fort have a pizza place?" he asked us.

I shook my head. "But it has a convenience store with frozen pizza and a microwave."

He talked to the travelers again.

They laughed some more and then shook hands with every one. Their grins were infectious, even Benjamin had to respond with a smile. They climbed into their car and drove off.

We all stood there for a minute.

"You didn't learn to speak German like that in a school class," Donavan said to Spence.

He shook his head. "We lived in Germany for six years. My dad was in the army. I went to an American school on the base, but I got to know a lot of German kids, too. It's easy to pick up a language when you're young. My dad speaks it, too." He looked embarrassed. "About as well as I do." He laughed. "At least, we haven't forgotten everything."

It was getting dark and no one seemed to feel like finishing the game.

"Your father was a career army man?" Donavan asked, and Spence nodded.

"He retired last year, but he isn't the type to loaf around. He had some good Navajo friends in the service. That's why he wanted to try his hand at running a store on the reservation. Also, he has asthma. It's not serious but the dry climate around here is good for him."

Spence laughed and looked around the group. "So, there you have my life's story . . . how I ended up in Carson's Crossing."

Boys started drifting off toward home. Only a few of us were left standing on the court.

"I can't believe those German guys," Donavan said. "Traveling all over the United States without knowing any English."

"Pretty daring, all right," Spence said.

"Pretty stupid, if you ask me," Benjamin said, bouncing the basketball.

We just looked at him.

"They should stay where they belong, with people who understand them," he said. He looked at Spence. "Everybody should be that smart."

He whirled around and walked off.

Donavan sighed. "Benjamin, you've got a lot to learn about the world outside of Carson's Crossing."

If Benjamin heard him, he didn't respond.

Chapter Seven

"What did you bring this time?" Anson asked.

"Cheese," David said.

"Again? We've tried that before."

David worked a small, plastic-wrapped lump from his jeans pocket. "Not this kind. They use this stuff on pizza."

My little brother and his best friend were going fishing, again. I couldn't help but envy them a little. They didn't worry whether being friends was *socially acceptable* or not. And, as a result, they had lots more fun than I did. I watched them disappear over the hill. I was going that way myself, but not for the fish.

That spring, Anson and David spent all their spare time together, usually down by the river. The water is muddy and warm and a few hearty catfish and carp hide in out-of-the-way places. The boys spent hours checking out different fishing holes and trying what they hoped would be tantalizing combinations for bait. The strangest was a tiny plastic soldier dipped in peanut butter. Although they didn't catch anything, being down there together seemed to be enough for them.

On that Friday in April, David finally caught a six-inch

carp. I have a feeling that the baby fish was too young to know about fishermen or it was snagged by accident, but there it was, flapping at the end of the line. I would have missed the great event if I hadn't been just around the bend with my sketch pad and water colors. There was a stand of tamarisk willows between us and I couldn't see the boys but, once in a while, I could hear them talking and laughing.

Suddenly, the talking turned into a shout.

"I've got one!" David yelled. "I'm not kidding this time, Anson. I've really got one!"

I decided to take a break from painting and check out the miracle. Sneaking through the willows, I hoped to have plenty to tease them about. Not just the size of the fish, no matter how big it was, but how they acted about catching it.

Sure enough, David was shouting and waving that fish as though it were a six-foot swordfish. Anson threw down his pole and came running.

"Nice catch!" he said.

Then a voice behind them sneered, "Well, look who's here."

Benjamin, Freeman, Alex, and Cecil were rounding the bend downstream. I ducked down.

"Looks like the Lone Ranger and his trusty sidekick, Tonto," laughed Cecil.

The younger boys recognized trouble when they saw it. Both of them focused their eyes on the ground, probably hoping the trouble would walk away. But it didn't. Instead, the older boys made a circle around them. I fought the impulse to head back to my paints.

Benjamin grabbed the fish out of David's hand.

"That's his fish, Benjamin!" Anson said. "Give it back!"

"You just shut up, little skunk," Benjamin told him in Navajo.

Then he turned to the others. In English, he said, "I heard that white men eat fish." He held the fish to his nose and sniffed. "I've even heard of people eating *raw* fish."

The others laughed and David shot a worried look to Anson.

"That's what I heard," continued Benjamin. "They start with the head and eat all the way to the tail."

"I've got to go home," David said with quivering lips. "My mom's expecting me for supper. You can just keep the fish."

"No need to hurry home to eat, white boy." Benjamin smiled. "There's plenty of supper right here."

He dangled the fish in front of David's face. The smaller boy made a break for it, but Freeman grabbed him and held him by the hair.

"Open wide, kid," Benjamin said. "You don't have to eat it, just bite off the head . . . you can just spit it out if you want to. Then, you can go home to momma, cry baby."

All of a sudden, I was on my feet, pushing through the willows.

"Leave them alone!" I shouted and all heads turned my direction.

"Don't get excited, Nelson," Benjamin said. "We aren't hurting your little brother. We're just having some fun with the white kid."

"Just quit messing around and let them go."

"I tried to get you to talk to him about showing some good taste in choosing friends." Benjamin smiled. "Anson's a Navajo, he should take some pride in that. Since you don't want to teach him or he doesn't want to listen to you, we're going to deliver the message.''

''I suppose he's going to see a lot to be proud of while he watches you brave warriors pick on little kids,'' I said. ''Just leave them alone.''

For sure, I'm no fighter. My heart was racing so fast I could feel it thumping. Pressure in my ears pushed the echo of my heart's thud into my head. Hoping the others wouldn't notice my shaking knees, I tried to keep my voice strong, but it cracked when I turned to Anson and David.

''Anson, Mom wants you home right now. David, you'd better go, too.''

''Not yet.'' Freeman grinned. ''He hasn't had his snack.''

He pulled David's head back by the hair and Benjamin laughed. All the details of the scene ricocheted through my mind: David's wince, Anson's helpless expression as his eyes went from his friend to me, Benjamin and Freeman's stupid laughter. In a flash, the heat of anger blasted through the fear that kept me frozen.

''You stupid jerk!'' I yelled and lunged for Freeman. I guess I surprised him because he let go of David as I hit him in the chest. Both of us went down.

The younger kids ran into the bushes and the bullies watched them disappear. Then, they walked over and helped Freeman up. I was really shaking now.

Freeman dusted off the seat of his pants. ''Hey, man, what's wrong with you?''

''Yeah, Nelson, are you nuts or something?'' asked Cecil.

Alex held out his hand to help me up. ''Somebody would think you liked that *Bilagaana* kid.''

''I just don't like to see little kids pushed around.''

"That's bull!" Benjamin said and the others looked at him. "You've never been Superman for younger kids before. You *do* like that West kid and you like his big brother, too."

A surprised look passed among the others.

"No matter where Nelson shows up, Spencer West is bound to show up sooner or later. I always see Nelson going to Gas and Goodies or coming from there," Benjamin explained. "Think about it, Nelson and old *Smells Like A Bear* are real buddies."

I wanted to say it wasn't true. I wanted to say, You're crazy, Benjamin Nez, Spencer West is nothing to me, but the words just wouldn't come.

"He's worse than a white man-loving traitor because he tries to hide it." Benjamin gave me a shove. "You phony . . . you lying phony!"

All of a sudden, I saw what Spence had been trying to explain all along. It's better to be yourself, stand up for the kids you want to call friends, no matter who they are, and face the consequences. At least that way, you don't feel like some kind of spineless wimp.

"We ought to beat the crap out of you for knocking down Freeman," Benjamin said.

"Go ahead and try it, you big, brave chickens. You're not picking on some elementary school kid now." I tried to sound tough, but all the time I was wishing that anger would come back to make me forget my shaking knees. "Do you want to try it one at a time or all four of you at once?"

"It won't take all of us to beat up one little white man-lover," Benjamin said, turning to Freeman. "This looks like your fight. Go ahead and finish it."

The rest of them backed away.

Freeman was bigger than me. He played football last

68

fall and still worked out in the weight room now and then to keep in shape. I knew I didn't have a chance. I thought about just standing there and letting him hit me a couple of times until I started bleeding, then the whole gang would probably leave me alone. If you fight back, you make the other guy madder and he hits harder.

"Freeman," I said, stalling. "Do you always take orders from Benjamin?"

Freeman stopped to think about what that meant.

"You have brains, man. Think for yourself. Don't just follow Benjamin around, letting him do all your thinking for you."

"I don't do that."

"Sure you do. In basketball, he tells you what position to play, who to pass the ball to, who to keep it away from."

He snorted a little laugh. "You're full of it!"

He hadn't hit me yet and I started feeling a little more confident, maybe I'd be able to talk my way out of this fight. We stood with our fists up, circling around, but no punches were thrown.

"If you let Benjamin give all the orders," I continued, "you're always going to be a big, dumb ox."

So much for talking my way out of a fight. I don't think Freeman understood my point, but he understood *big, dumb ox*. He came at me in one fast blur, slugging me in the lip. I fell backwards and my head thudded against the dirt.

I guess it was the fastest fight in history. As I lay there with blood making a little line from my mouth toward my ear, Freeman turned and joined the others. They walked toward the tamarisk willows, then Benjamin turned back to me.

"That's just a taste of what could happen to phony liars who think pushy white kids are more important than their old friends."

He said the rest in Navajo. "It's not too late. We're still your friends if you stop acting crazy and get rid of your white dog."

Then they were gone.

I lay there for a minute and then walked back to the watercolor set I'd left next to the river. Carefully, I washed the blood from my lip and chin. The cool water felt good so I kept splashing it on my face even after the blood was gone. That's where Spence found me.

"Are you okay?" he asked. "David came running in crying about how you saved him from some big bullies. He said they were beating you up. I left him in charge of the store and took off as soon as I could make sense of his directions for finding you."

I smiled at him and winced a little. "It's nothing, just a misunderstanding."

"Looks like the misunderstanding used a right hook." It was his turn to smile. Then, he grew serious. "I just want you to know you are some friend, Nelson Sam. That was really something, standing up for David against that gang like you did."

I laughed, thinking back to my thumping heart and shaking knees.

We didn't talk as I gathered up my painting materials, but I'd tell him all about it on the way home. At least I'd taken a stand. I didn't deny that the Wests were my friends and I didn't run away from the fight. A strong feeling of relief flooded through me. Maybe it was the fact that I was alive, but I think it came from knowing I didn't have to be shadowman any longer.

Carefully, I touched the corner of my lip and it stung a little. I was feeling so courageous that even the sting felt good.

Chapter Eight

I never exactly made the announcement, "Spence West and I are now best friends," but I stopped hiding it. To my surprise, to my embarrassment, the only thing that changed was that we went places together instead of scheduling separate arrival and departure times. At school, even at the youth center, the way people acted toward us was the same. The mistreatment from Benjamin and his friends that I'd worried about never came. Benjamin and his gang remained as cool and insulting to Spence as ever and they ignored me just like they always had. Their threat to get me was never put into action. Maybe they were just waiting for the right time.

The first Saturday in May, Spence came over to see if I wanted to go down to the river. He was trying to fill his sketch pad for art class. He could always count on my willingness to go along; helping him with art assignments was a perfect excuse to escape work at home.

"*Iniyaa'ish?*" my mom asked him. "Did you eat breakfast?"

Old Walks Like A Bear had become a member of our family.

"I just finished a big breakfast, but thanks anyway," Spence said.

"Have a piece of toast then." My mother never accepted *no* as a final answer where food was concerned.

"Put some peanut butter and honey on it," Anson suggested.

So Spence crunched on a toast while the rest of us finished the scrambled eggs, fried potatoes and bacon.

"No playing for me today," I said, taking my plate to the sink.

He looked disappointed.

"It's shearing time. I have to go to Grandma's and help with the sheep."

"That sounds fun," Spence said.

"That's what you think." I laughed.

"It's hard, smelly work," my dad said, "but if you want to come with us, I'm sure we could use an extra hand."

"Even an inexperienced *white* hand," I said.

My mother gave her usual gasp and shook her head, but *white* and *red man* jokes were a regular part of our conversations.

"Thanks," Spence said. "It will only take a minute to ask my mom. I'm all ready to go."

"Oh, no, you're not," I said. "Go home and get into your oldest, grubbiest clothes. Then, you'll be ready."

Spence raced home to change. In a few minutes we drove our old brown pickup to the store to get him.

"Can I bring my camera?" Spence asked as we pulled up.

"Of course," my dad said.

As Spence settled down in the pickup bed with Russell, Anson, and me, he said, "I read that Navajos don't like to have their pictures taken."

"Where did you read that?" I asked.

"A book my dad just brought home."

"How old's the book? That ancient stuff has been gone for a long time," Russell said. "Well, I guess, there might be some superstitious Navajos still left, holding onto the idea that a photograph captures the soul of the person in the picture. But you don't have to worry about that with our family. We're modern."

I laughed. "You can tell by our fancy transportation."

The old truck rattled onto the road, picking up speed.

"We use only the finest bubble gum to keep it together," Russell continued. Everybody laughed because we knew about the automotive magic my dad performed with baling wire and pieces of inner tube.

Riding in the back of a pickup truck down reservation roads is a real adventure. I could see why Yvonne and Rosemary insisted on sitting in the front with Mom and Dad. It's dusty and loud back there and you have to shout to carry on a conversation.

In a bellow, I taught Spence some Navajo phrases to use with my grandmother. Navajo is hard enough to say when you're talking quietly. Poor Spence was bouncing along, shouting into the whipping wind. Pretty soon, everybody in the pickup bed was laughing and yelling encouragement to Spence. We had a great time.

When we pulled up in front of my grandmother's hogan, we could see her through the open door, waiting inside. We knocked on the door frame anyway and she told us to come in. That's Navajo manners, to wait until you're invited in, even at your grandma's house.

A hogan is a round log house with mud heaped on the roof. It's the very best kind of house for our country. Because of all the dirt heaped around it, it's warm in the winter and cool in the summer. When some people think about a mud home, they get the picture of a cave but my grandma is very fussy. She even dusts the crisscrossed logs of the ceiling.

As we went in, I looked around with a new perspective, wondering what Spence was thinking. On nails hammered into the logs were pans and coats, a pair of tennis shoes, the bridle for Grandma's old horse. On the ceiling logs, over the bed and table and stove, Grandma had stretched pieces of bright cotton cloth to catch any dirt that might sift down from the roof. Every morning, after she does the dishes, my grandmother sweeps the dirt floor and then sprinkles the rinse water around to settle the dust and harden the floor. The dirt is as hard as cement.

Grandma was sitting near the middle of the hogan cleaning pinto beans for the meal later on. In cold weather an empty fifty-gallon oil drum with a door cut in its side would stand where she was sitting. A chimney coming from the top would extend upward, going out the roof of the hogan. Since it was almost summer, the drum stove was gone and a shaft of sunlight slid through the smoke hole, spilling across Grandma's lap so she could see the beans better. The cooking stove was next to the door, and next to that stood an old wooden cupboard. Grandma's bed was across from the door next to the wall. Here and there were chairs and boxes to use as chairs for today's visitors.

Spencer went over to my grandmother and shook her hand. *"Ya'at'eeh, Shimasani,"* he said. The greeting, "Hello, Grandmother," is a show of respect. You don't have to be related to use it. In the Navajo way, you address any elderly woman as "Grandmother."

She said, *"Ya'at'eeh."*

"Spencer yinishye," he said, just like I'd coached him. My grandmother nodded at his introduction of himself.

74

"You have a nice home," Spencer said like a pro.

My grandmother nodded again and smiled.

Then Spence just stood there. He couldn't think of any more Navajo to say, his store phrases just wouldn't fit. The silence was very loud, growing louder by the second, and Anson stifled a giggle.

"I think we might become friends faster . . ." my grandmother's voice sliced through the quiet air, "if we spoke English."

Spencer looked up at me quickly. He grinned, realizing he'd been the target of another joke. Then everybody laughed.

"Nelson didn't tell me you spoke English, Mrs. Benally."

"Nelson always teases," Grandma said. "I learned English a long time ago at boarding school . . . I think I was around eight years old."

"I almost had to go to boarding school when I was twelve. Luckily, my dad got transferred. I was so scared about leaving home," Spence said.

"I was scared, too, when government men came to give me a ride to the school, but they thought they were doing a good thing. They knew that we had to learn new things if we were going to change with the world. I learned many things: numbers and strange places in the world . . ." She smiled. " 'She'll Be Coming 'Round the Mountain' and the 'Virginia Reel'. . . . And English, English was very important. . . . In those days, if we talked Navajo at school, they spanked us."

"That's terrible."

"Maybe not. We learned pretty good English." She took the beans to the table. "I don't talk it much, just a little."

"It was evil *Bilagaanas* that kidnapped you and took

you to school, wasn't it, Grandma?" Russell asked, looking over at Spence.

Grandma laughed. "No, grandson, you know it was Navajos and they weren't evil. They were just doing their job."

Spence grinned at Russell. "Evil *Bilagaanas* . . ."

"Many things they taught us at that school I don't use," my grandmother went on. "But now school is important. My grandsons must learn everything."

"I'm sure they will." Spence looked directly into her eyes.

"They will if they work hard, but if they spend all their time teasing . . ."

Russell started toward the door before she finished. "Let's get busy!"

Grandma, Mom and my younger sisters started fixing the afternoon meal. It would take a long time to prepare, but we had lots of work to keep us busy until it was ready. Spence grabbed his camera from the back of the pickup and we followed Dad and Russell to the shed behind the sheep corral. My Uncle Alfred was already shearing.

I introduced him to Spence. He just looked up and said, "*Ya'at'eeh*." He was crouched over a sheep, holding its hind legs still with his own legs. Carefully, he used the old-fashioned sheep shears to clip the wool off in long, even strips. Because my uncle has been shearing for years, he gets right to the sheep's skin.

"I clip close so the sheep won't be too hot this summer," he explained.

"He's just saying that, Spence," my dad said with a smile. "He's thinking about getting as much wool as he can so he'll get more money when he sells it."

Uncle Alfred laughed. When he finished the sheep, he stood up, stretched the muscles in his back, and offered his hand. Spence clasped it in a gentle Navajo handshake. When Aunt Irene came in a few minutes later, he shook her hand, too. Shaking hands is another important part of Navajo manners.

Spence asked permission and then snapped a few pictures of the shearing process. As the day went on, he took other pictures of the work we did. Believe me, we worked! Sometimes we held sheep while the older folks sheared. Sometimes we took armfuls of wool to the big bags in the corner. When a bag was full, we tied it tightly with string and took it to the back of the pickup. From noon on, the little shed got hotter and hotter but we kept working. I think Spence found out my dad wasn't kidding when he said it was sweaty work.

At four o'clock, just before we ate, my father asked Spence if he wanted to shear one of the last sheep.

"Sure," he said, "I'll give it a try."

The men brought in a sheep and held it down. Spence took the shears and started to cut off the wool. "Nelson, take some pictures of this historical event," he said.

I snapped a couple of photos.

"Oops!" he said when he knicked the sheep's skin. "This is harder than it looks."

"These pictures may become evidence when the humane society tries to put you in prison," I teased.

Spence's tongue crept out at the corner of his mouth as he concentrated on the shears.

"Oops!" he said again.

"I think we'd better change your name to Skins Like A Wolf," Anson said seriously and everybody laughed.

About five inches and six *oops* later, Spence gave up and handed the shears to Alfred.

"Poor sheep," he said. "It probably thinks it's been

butchered instead of shorn. I'm sorry. I hope I didn't hurt it.''

"After a few hundred sheep, you'll be a pro," I said. "But I hope you don't want to start your training right now. I'm starved! Let's go wash up for supper."

We ate in my Aunt Irene's house because it's bigger than Grandma's. But the food had been prepared in the hogan so it tasted terrific. We had pinto beans boiled with bacon until the juice was dark pink, broiled goat ribs, fried potatoes and onions, fry bread, and more.

"This fry bread tastes a lot like the scones my mom makes," Spence said. "Only better, of course." He winked at Grandma.

Finally, we couldn't eat any more. Spencer leaned back and sighed. "I think I need a bigger belt. Thank you, Mrs. Benally. That's the best meal I've ever eaten."

Grandma smiled. "You earned it. You worked hard all day."

When the time came for us to go back to Carson's Crossing, Spencer shook hands with my grandmother again.

He said, "*Hagoone.*" Just like I'd taught him.

Grandma held his hand for a moment.

"*Hagoone, shiyazh,*" she said. "I like you, Spence. I don't know too many white people, but you are like my family. It's nice you came to help. Come again, *shiyazh.* You are welcome any time."

Spence said goodbye to Irene and Alfred, then went to the pickup. When I climbed in next to him, he was just staring at the bed of the truck.

"You must be all worn out," I said.

"I feel great!"

"You must also have a few loose wires in your brain."

"It's not that I feel so terrific physically, Nelson. I am

78

tired," he answered. "I just feel this funny warm feeling on the inside."

"Maybe you have a fever."

"What did your grandmother call me? '*Shiyazh?*' . . . What's that?"

"It means *my son*, only it's a little more than that. It's hard to translate into English. It means *little one* but it carries a special, tender feeling."

"*Shiyazh*," he said to himself.

I punched him playfully on the arm. "You should feel like something special happened. My grandmother calling you, '*shiyazh*' is like the Queen of England making you a knight. Grandma doesn't accept many people on the very first meeting."

Chapter Nine

I don't usually listen to other people's conversations. It happened by accident. I could blame it on Mrs. Bolton, my English teacher, or even on Benjamin and his friends for talking so loud.

Thinking back, I'm sure the trouble started at lunch and grew from there. Spence brought his pictures of the sheep shearing to school and we were looking at them as we ate.

Spence held up one of the pictures I'd taken. "Is it a bird? A plane? No, it's Super Shearer!"

I laughed. "It looks to me like you're working for the Beef Council, trying to eliminate all sheep from the face of the earth."

Spence laughed with me.

"What's so funny?" Benjamin and his gang were hanging over our backs, looking down at the photos.

"We took some pictures out at Nelson's grandma's house last week," Spence said.

"And you think the way she lives is so funny?"

"Wait a minute, we aren't laughing at . . ."

"Just like a white man." Benjamin turned to the others. "He pushes his way into some place he doesn't belong and then makes fun of what he finds there."

"I wasn't making fun of anything," Spence began.

"Spence tried to sheer a sheep . . ." I started to explain.

"We don't need to hear any more, Nelson, you skunk head. You're worse than the Gas and Goodies boy here. You take him out to your family's home and then laugh with him when he ridicules it."

I stood up. "Listen, you guys, we weren't ridiculing any . . ."

They turned and walked away, and we watched them swagger through the door.

"I guess they don't want to get the story straight," I said.

"If they got the story straight, they wouldn't have any reason to be mad. I don't think they want to take that chance." Spence collected the photos and put them in his pocket. "I'm beginning to understand the warning you gave me about those guys on the first day I came here, Nelson."

"Pretty slow learner, aren't you?" I said. "I guess we can just blame it on your *Bilagaana* genes."

Spence looked at his pants. "These are made in Korea."

We laughed at the dumb joke just to chase away the ugly feeling Benjamin had left behind.

Mrs. Bolton is in charge of the yearbook. Whenever she needs some extra time to work on it, she sends the kids in her English classes to the library for a study period. Nobody uses the hour for study.

Sure enough, that afternoon Mrs. Bolton had a yearbook emergency and I ended up in the library. I decided to find a book that Spencer said had some startling old pictures from Fort Sumner and was searching a bottom shelf when

I heard Benjamin's voice in the next aisle. I started to back away, who wants to spend free time in a hassle, but something caught my ear.

". . . no real rough stuff. Just mess things up a little and have a few laughs."

"That white man is thinking he can go anywhere he pleases." The voice sounded like Freeman. "He even goes out to Nelson's grandmother's place now."

"And then makes fun of her and the way Navajos live," someone finished.

I decided I had to hear a little more so I leaned closer.

"Tonight is Lion's Club. Both his father and mother will go because they're planning for the Fourth of July. We'll have plenty of time. When they go, they always leave Spencer at the store to take care of things."

Alex laughed. "Only tonight, we'll be the ones taking care of things."

I'd heard enough so I moved slowly toward the end of the aisle. I guess Benjamin was leaving too because, just as I got to the end of the shelves, he got to the end of his aisle."

His eyes widened in surprise, then narrowed. "Nelson, *sik'is!*" He smiled but it didn't look like he meant the *my friend* part.

I'm sure my face went red. It usually does when I'm caught at something.

"How long have you been there?"

"Huh? . . . Just a second. It's the wrong shelf," I stammered. "I'm . . . I'm looking for the . . . animal books."

Benjamin started pushing me back down the aisle toward the wall. "Doing a report on snakes?" he said. "Or skunks? You should know a lot about them, they're your kind."

I looked around for Ms. Benally, the librarian. Any other time she would have been right at my elbow, telling me to be more quiet, but she was nowhere in sight.

They crowded me down to the end of the aisle and pinned me next to the wall.

"Listen, white man-lover, we aren't going to do anything to hurt anybody. We just want your best buddy, Spencer West, to know how we feel about whites. He just keeps pushing into Navajo places—our places." Benjamin was standing really close to me as he talked. He had a pinch of Skoal snuff between his lip and his gum, and his teeth had flakes of tobacco on them. I could smell the wintergreen odor as he spit out the words. "Your white friend not only crowded into the youth center, but now he wants to start up the Indian Club again. We just want him to stay where he belongs—out of our territory."

Spence had been talking about the Indian Club for weeks. I kept discouraging him, but I guess he'd gone ahead and talked to Mr. Toledo about it.

Freeman interrupted. "There's gonna be no real hurting. Just enough to give him the message."

"Listen, you guys," I said desperately. "You'd like Spence if you gave him a chance. Just meet him halfway. There's nothing wrong with him."

"Just one thing," Johnny said, "he's white."

Benjamin leaned over and poked his finger into my chest to emphasize his words. "If something messes up our plans, we'll know who told about it. We'll know exactly how you feel about your own people."

He leaned very close to me. "Turning traitor will introduce you to a whole new world of enemies, Nelson. Your little brother and sisters won't be too popular either. Think about it."

They left me leaning against the bookshelf, feeling like

I might throw up. I didn't know if I was scared or just sick about Spence's trouble.

I knew what I should do, but I just kept thinking about what they'd said. Change my whole life. Except for Spence, the white kids stayed in their own group. The Navajo kids would ignore me if Benjamin put some pressure on them. So what? I thought. I like being on my own.

What about Anson and Yvonne and Rosemary? My mind started whirling. Anson was spoiled and kind of a baby but he had David for a friend. I wasn't too worried about him. Yvonne was in sixth grade. Her friends were the most important thing in her life. First grader Rosemary wasn't big enough to take care of herself if other kids picked on her. Benjamin had a little brother. Cecil had a younger sister. Alex had a million little kids in his family. What if they got the kids at the elementary school to take out their revenge on my sisters? Could they survive like I could? I had Spence but they had nobody.

The questions kept bouncing around in my mind. Benjamin had said that nobody would get hurt. It was just a prank. It wasn't as though they were going to blow up the store or shoot somebody. Spence could handle it. I knew he could handle anything. He'd talk them out of it. He'd probably buy them a pop and show them that he wasn't just a *white man*, but a real person. He could do it. I knew he could. Anyway, the wimp in me whispered, how would he ever find out that I'd overheard the plan? Sure, that was the way to handle things.

I'd made a decision but the problem just wouldn't be settled. Like a restless dog, the worry kept whining at my mind, pawing at my attention, instead of curling up in a corner and going to sleep.

After school, walking home with Spence, I felt like I'd

been fighting grizzly bears. He kept the conversation going but he had to repeat every question and settle for one-syllable answers when I finally responded.

"Is anything wrong?" Spence asked at last.

"No! Why so many questions?" I snapped and immediately regretted it. "I just . . . I'm just a little tired."

"Do you want to stop at my place for milk and cookies?" He always asked and we always stopped. Today, I didn't feel hungry.

I had an idea. "How about going over to the center and shooting a few baskets?" I suggested. Maybe, if we got in a good game with Benjamin and the others, they'd forget their plans. It was a long shot but maybe . . .

"I'd better not, Nelson," Spence said. "I've got to watch the store tonight while my folks go to Lion's Club. I want to get my homework done before then. Thanks, anyway."

"Maybe I will have some cookies." I was stalling for time to think of a way to warn him without bringing trouble to my little sisters.

Mrs. West was placing peanut butter cookies on a serving tray when we walked in.

"Refreshments for the Lion's Club," she explained. "You boys take the ones over there that are broken or funny shaped."

"They taste just as good." Spence brought glasses of milk to the table then reached for the plate of rejects.

I brought a cookie to my mouth, then a desperate thought flashed into my head. "Baking all these cookies was a lot of work, Mrs. West. Maybe you should take the night off and stay home."

She looked over at me in surprise. "I couldn't do that. At least, not tonight. We're planning the activities for the

85

Fourth of July. It seems a long way off, but there's plenty of work to fill up that time.''

"I . . . I just thought maybe the store might be too busy for Spence to handle.''

Now, they both looked at me like I was some kind of lunatic.

"On a Thursday?'' Spence snorted. "You've got to be kidding.''

They watched me finish my milk; I couldn't eat the cookie. Then Spence followed me to the door. "Are you all right?'' he asked.

"Sure . . . it's just that. . . .'' Words became trapped in my throat, held down by a big knot in my stomach.

He waited.

"Never mind,'' I said and walked away. When I looked back, Spence was still watching me.

After dragging myself home, I moped around trying to decide what to do. I wanted to talk to my dad but it seemed that the problem would just get bigger if I spread it to other people. Maybe I was afraid he'd tell me to do what I knew a best friend should do.

Sitting at the dinner table, poking ham casserole and corn around my plate, and listening to Rosemary and Yvonne chatter about their friends didn't help me find a solution to my problem.

Finally, it dawned on me that I didn't have to warn Spence, I just had to be around to help him if things got out of hand. By the time I thought of that, it was too late. Spence told me later what happened.

Benjamin, Freeman, Johnny, Alex, and Cecil came into the store, just after Mr. and Mrs. West left. The guys must have been watching.

Spence was surprised to see them, but he said "Hi''

and asked if he could help them find anything. They didn't answer, just wandered up and down the aisles in the store. There's really no way to swear in Navajo but they kept muttering insults in low, ugly voices.

Benjamin stopped and picked up a bag of sugar. He swung the bag against the edge of the shelf and sugar poured down onto the floor. "Oops!" he said with a grin.

"What's the big idea, Benjamin?" Spence asked.

"No idea," snarled Freeman. "We just want to show you that when people go where they shouldn't, it makes a mess of things."

He slowly pushed a jar of honey to the edge of the shelf and watched it crash to the floor.

"That's enough!" Spencer's voice rose higher. "I don't know what you think you're proving by this dumb stunt but you ought to go home."

"Just so you understand, white man," Benjamin said as he picked up a dozen eggs. Holding the open carton high in the air, he slowly turned it upside down and let the eggs splatter on the floor.

As the last egg hit the linoleum, Spence leaped over the counter and grabbed Cecil, who happened to be closest. He pushed him into the ice cream case, knocking over the carefully stacked bottles of topping and boxes of cones that were on top. Then he went for Benjamin.

Benjamin started to meet him, but forgot about the broken eggs. Slipping across the floor, he grabbed a shelf, and it came down on top of him. The shelf was full of pancake flour and syrup. Some of the bags of flour caught on the shelf as it clattered to the floor and spilled out. Other bags split open when they hit the ground. One bottle of syrup hit the bottom shelf and broke. Syrup oozed out over Benjamin's lap. Two more syrup bottles were broken, forming small brown lakes in the aisle.

The other boys ran to the door, stopping to help Cecil up. Benjamin was the only one left, looking up into Spence's angry face.

"I hope you're finished," Spence said, getting control. "I hope you can go home now and feel proud of yourself."

Benjamin looked around in astonishment. "Hey, man, we didn't mean to make such a mess." He got up slowly. Pancake flour slid down his chest to powder the syrup that was dripping down his legs. He picked up an unbroken bottle of syrup and started to set it back on the shelf. When it dawned on him there was no shelf, he put it carefully on the floor. "I mean, we weren't going to make this big of a mess, you know," he said.

"Just get out of here," Spence said and went to the back room to get a broom, some rags and the mop-bucket so he could clean things up.

When he came back, Benjamin was gone and I was standing there, looking at the shelf and the mess on the floor.

"Our friends were just here." Spence set down his cleaning equipment. "Too bad you missed the party."

"Man, I'm sorry, Spence."

"It's not your fault. Grab the end of that shelf, will you? Maybe we can get this mess cleaned up before my dad gets home. If he finds out, his army temper will flare up and he'll want to prosecute those guys. I just want it to be over, now."

We manuevered the shelf back into place and Spence wiped it clean. He spoke as he worked. "I think they just wanted to make some kind of statement and pushing me around made it for them. Maybe they learned something. I think they didn't plan on making this big of a mess."

As we stacked the unbroken bags and bottles on the

shelf, I kept trying to think of words, words that would bring my feelings out into the light, words that were stronger than *sorry* and *ashamed*.

"I know I learned something," Spence went on. "You can't really change other people, you can't make them into what you want them to be. Maybe, if you hit them in the head with a tire iron, they'll change for a few minutes, but going out of your way to be friendly to someone doesn't guarantee they'll be friendly back."

Working side-by-side with Spence, I watched the confusion of glass and flour and egg shells getting wiped up and sorted and put in the right place. A sense of order slowly moved into the physical space around me. But words were still careening through my brain cells, phrases crashing into one another and bouncing apart. The problem wasn't just in my head; there was a sick feeling in my chest. It was like a small animal had crawled in there and died, its carcass decaying and bloating. If I could have drawn a picture, maybe I would've found a way to show Spence my betrayal and help him understand, but words were so hard.

Finally, the store was back to its usual, military perfection. I knew I had to at least try to straighten up the mess inside of me.

"I'm sorry," I said. "I could have helped, Spence. I was going to help. That's why I came over here."

He looked bewildered.

I hurried on, afraid I might choke on the words or, worse, push them back down my throat unsaid. "I knew . . . I knew they were coming here. I've known it all day."

Emotions marched across his face in a silent, terrible parade: disbelief, then understanding and acknowledgment, a split second of hurt, followed by searing anger.

"You knew? You knew those guys were coming here,

89

looking for a fight?'' He clenched his fists and I thought he might punch me. I hoped he would. Slug me, Spence, bloody my lip, break my nose. You'll feel better. *I'll* feel better.

"Nelson, you're such a. . . . Man, that's really great. Get out of here!'' Grabbing my shirt, he shoved me toward the door. "Go join your stupid friends . . . follow your buddies!''

It would have been easy to walk away, but I turned back, stammering about Rosemary . . . Yvonne . . . the threats Benjamin had made in the library at school.

As I talked, Spence's fists relaxed and his angry expression slipped away. The more frightening expression, hurt, staggered back onto his face for a second time. Suddenly, I recognized all my reasons for what they were, just excuses. I was scared and I'd let that fear keep me from being a friend.

Spence's eyes were bright as his shoulders slumped. "I guess what I told you about changing people goes for friends, too, Nelson. I made the same mistake with you that I made with Benjamin and the others. I bullied you into friendship. You said you didn't want it and I kept pushing and begging. I was like a little kid whining to go on a super, grownups-only roller coaster. Once he's on, he knows how stupid it was to force the issue.''

He picked up the bucket and walked toward the back room. At the end of the aisle, he turned to me. "I'm sorry, *sik'is*. I knew something was wrong with our friendship, but I didn't know how serious it was. Friends help friends, Nelson Sam. Real friends stick together.''

He disappeared into the back. After a few seconds I went out the front door. What could I say to that?

90

Chapter Ten

The evening air was cool and I shivered. I felt like I should cry, or throw up, or run till my heavy, painful breathing drowned out the voices in my head, but it took every molecule of my disappearing energy to pick up one foot, set it down a few inches ahead, then pick up the other foot.

Sunsets are one part of Carson's Crossing that are spectacular. As I stared into the layers of light—canary and tangarine and vermilion, fading into rose and mauve, eventually swallowed by indigo—I tried to settle the day's events in my mind. I had thought that telling Spence would clear my conscience, but I didn't feel better. My best friend hated me.

I straightened my shoulders. So what? Everything worked out perfectly, just the way I'd wanted all along. I was a free agent again. No more worry about being the center of attention. This was great!

Then, why didn't I feel better? Instead of a weight sliding from my shoulders, it seemed like a few extra tons had been added. Even worse, I had to carry the load by myself.

I already missed Spencer West. I thought of his laugh,

the way he could always think of something fun to do, the teasing he dished out and accepted all the time. I thought of the crazy way his eyes lit up when he called himself Walks Like A Bear. I wanted my best friend back.

A crazy thought flew into my head and, right away, I felt better. What was keeping me from repairing that friendship? I could pester Spence into being best friends again. After all, I'd had the best teacher in the world, old Walks Like A Bear, himself! I'd start tomorrow.

Patching things up took longer than I thought. I planned to start bugging him first thing in the morning so he'd be worn down by lunch, but Spence avoided me all day. I couldn't find him in the halls or the lunchroom. Even in classes we had together, he managed to be deep in conversation with someone else when I came along.

By the time the last bell rang, I'd decided that I'd make one try with the direct approach. I hid behind the pop machine until Spence was at his locker. Then I marched over and grabbed him by the arm, turning him to face me.

"I'm sorry I was a jerk and I want to be friends again," I said the way I'd rehearsed it all day.

He just looked at me so I tried again. "Do you want to be my friend or do you want to forget the whole thing?"

"Yes."

"Yes? What does that mean?" I was still confused. "Yes, we're still friends or yes, forget it?"

"Yes, let's be friends," he said and grinned.

It was that simple. He didn't make me sign any oath of loyalty. He didn't have some complicated ritual to make us blood brothers. He grinned and I grinned and we were best friends again, instantly.

We walked out of Manuelito High into the gentle spring breeze and headed for the river.

"Do you want to go to the youth center today?" I asked.

He just kept walking.

"Our team will be expecting us to help them win the game," I explained.

He laughed. "I know a few who might be expecting us with their bows and arrows ready."

We walked in silence for a moment.

"I don't know, Nelson," Spence said. "I've done a lot of thinking since last night. I can see why Benjamin and his friends think I'm always pushing into their business. I'm going to stay away from the center for a while. You know better than anyone that I can use that time to practice my drawing for art."

"You can't do that," I said and he looked at me. "If you practice drawing as hard as you play basketball, you might get good at it, better than me. Anybody knows that too much competition can ruin a friendship."

He snorted. "You don't have to worry, Van Gogh."

"Sorry, I can't take that chance." I set my backpack under a tree and sat down, leaning against it. Spence followed my lead.

"The thing is, Spencer West, if you don't show up at the center today, you just won't be you. You'll be a shadowman, like me . . . like I *was* . . . like I'm trying not to be. I say we go play basketball and just be ourselves. If some people don't like it, that's their problem. They just have to be themselves, too."

Spence dug some mud out of the grooves in the bottom of his sneaker. "And if being themselves means they have to beat the tar out of us? . . ."

I shrugged. "They'll have to catch us first."

"Make sure your shoes are tied."

"So, what do you say?"

93

"I say you are very brave, Nelson Sam," Spence said, ". . . or very crazy. Either way . . . I'm with you."

We hurried home to change, then Spence came by my place and we went to the center together. Both of us were expecting trouble, but it never came.

Maybe, as Spence said, the Benjamin gang just had to make some kind of statement, get some twisted resentment out of their systems. Whatever it was, the next week was quiet, like a truce. Choosing teams became less rigid, and we mixed ourselves up more so that everyone got a better chance to pass and shoot.

Sometimes Spence was with Benjamin and sometimes not. After seeing Benjamin smile a couple of times when Spence made a crucial basket for his team, I started to think that there might be hope for burying the hatchet, as they say. I was optimistic that, when the time came, Benjamin wouldn't bury it in Spence's head.

During the ceasefire, our basketball skills improved a lot. No matter how the teams came out when we were choosing sides, we worked together. Benjamin's friends stopped worrying about offending him and started thinking of Spence as a member of their team. Even Benjamin seemed to become color-blind when we were on the court.

All this cooperation was great! Then, Spence had to open his big mouth.

We were in gym on Thursday, toward the end of May and Mr. Stark, our regular teacher, was gone. Mr. Stark is also the baseball coach for Manuelito High. Lucky for us, Mr. Tsinnijinnie was substituting for Coach Stark. He was letting everybody play basketball. I know that's strange for May, but Tsinnijinnie is the basketball coach, and he likes to scout early for next year's team. We'd been practicing baseball skills since February and were sick of playing it, so this was a welcome change.

The shower bell rang and we headed for the locker room.

"Spence, how did you learn to play like that?" Bruce Maxfield asked.

Spence shrugged. "I once shook hands with Larry Bird."

Bruce grinned. "That's the whole secret?"

"I also sleep in a Dr. J. tee-shirt."

"You ought to come up to the plant and practice with us sometime."

I looked over at Spence as we stopped at our lockers to undress and get towels.

"Bruce, by the time I walked up to the Texaco plant," Spence said, "I wouldn't have enough energy to play ball."

"My mom will pick you up."

"Thanks, anyway, but I've got a team I play with."

"You do?"

"I practice over at the youth center."

Bruce stopped trying to open the padlock on his locker and looked over at Spence. "At the mission with Indian kids?"

"That's the place." Spence took off his shoes and socks and put them away. He was pulling off his tee-shirt when Bruce spoke again and had to have him repeat his question.

"I said, are those guys any good?"

"Any good in general terms, as people, or as basketball players?"

"Basketball players, of course."

"With me on their team, they never lose." Spence laughed at his own boast.

After wrapping his towel around his waist, Bruce headed down the aisle toward the showers. He stopped and turned back. "Of course, you guys haven't played a real team yet."

"What's a real team?"

"The Wildcats, our Texaco team." Bruce grinned. "If you played us, your team would soften up and sag like marshmallows at a camp-out."

I pushed into the conversation. "You guys would have to light a fire first." I grabbed my towel and followed Spence toward the showers, passing Bruce. "You wouldn't even get your matches lit because we'd keep running past you so fast that the wind would blow them out."

"Oh, yeah?"

Spence cut in. "There's only one way to find out. How about a game Saturday morning?"

"Spence," I said softly. "Hadn't we better ask the other guys about it?"

"You're on!" Bruce said. "See you at ten o'clock. We'll even give you the home court advantage . . . unless your team is still shooting at a bushel basket with the bottom knocked out."

"Very funny, hot shot. See you Saturday. Bring plenty of Gatorade and Ben-gay."

Bruce just laughed and went down to the shower head at the end.

"Are you nuts?" I asked as we lathered up. "Benjamin is going to kill you . . . us."

"Why? We can beat Texaco's team."

"In the first place, he hates those guys."

"All of them?"

"Most of them."

"There must be some Navajos on that team."

I nodded. "A few, but Benjamin calls them Oreos."

"Oreos?"

"Like the cookies, brown on the outside but white inside. He says they've sold out and spend their time trying to be white."

In a minute, Spence finished rinsing off and grabbed his towel. "Doesn't Benjamin's dad work for Texaco?"

"Yes, but they don't live up in Texaco housing."

I followed him back to the lockers. "Benjamin doesn't have anything to do with those Texaco kids, Navajo or white."

Spence grinned. "Then it's time he had something to do with them, even if it's just one basketball game. He'll be glad we gave him the opportunity."

"That brings me to the second reason for not doing what you just did," I said. "Benjamin is going to hate the idea of this game because he didn't think of it—he wasn't the one to issue the challenge."

Spence laughed.

I just couldn't bring myself to join him. "I don't know what Benjamin is going to say about this grudge match on Saturday, but I bet it's going to be loud."

"You idiot!" Benjamin yelled. "Who made you the boss of the center?" He threw the ball hard against the wall of the mission and caught it. "It must be in a white man's blood to take over everything."

"Let's be cool," Josh said. Benjamin shot him a quick and deadly glance.

"Right," Donavan said. "This might turn out to be a good thing. I've been watching you guys. You're ready for some competition. You could beat Texaco's team with all your legs in casts."

"Of course, we could," Benjamin said. "I just hate having all that *Bilagaana* sweat messing up our court."

Everybody laughed.

97

Freeman said, "It might be fun to beat them to a pulp."

"Figuratively speaking," Josh added.

"They'll show up in those fancy uniforms, and we'll walk out in our old gym shorts," Alex said.

"At least we can get in a few baskets while they're laughing." My attempt to keep things light.

"Uniforms don't matter. It's your talent and drive that wins games," Donavan said.

"For a minute there, you gave a very good impression of a real coach," Spence teased.

"Let's hope he is," Benjamin said. "We can't back out now."

As Alex predicted, Texaco arrived in shiny, red-and-white satin uniforms. Benjamin was calling the plays for our team and Bruce Maxfield seemed to be captain of the Wildcats. The game started out like a cowboys and Indian movie. Texaco had only Anglos on the court, and Spence was warming the bench for us. Josh was keeping time and Donavan and Mr. Maxfield, Bruce's father, were referees.

Each team had planned to start fast and get an early lead, so the score remained close through the first quarter. During the second quarter, both teams kept changing players to try and find some advantage. The Wildcats had to bring out some Navajo players because they needed their quickness and stamina. Although he was trying most of the shots and making quite a few baskets, Benjamin finally called on Spence to help us narrow Texaco's eight-point lead.

Our campfire picture of the game turned out to be a little tame. We should have used fireworks as a comparison. Johnny and Cecil both fouled out in the third quarter, and we felt the loss. Benjamin kept calling for the ball, but he had Wildcats all over him so the ball went to

Spence more often. He consistently made the basket. I could see that Benjamin was getting steamed, but I didn't know if he was mad at the Texaco players or Spence.

With a few seconds left, the Wildcats led by two points. We had the ball, and the best we could hope for was a basket to tie us into overtime. We worked the ball down the court as carefully as time would allow.

"Nelson!" I heard Benjamin's insistent call. There was no clear pass to him. Spence was well-covered, too. I could almost hear the timer clicking in my head. The time was going, going . . . As Benjamin ran back downcourt into the clear, Spence dodged quickly under the basket, breaking free of his guards.

"Nelson!" Benjamin yelled again.

I threw the ball to Spence. The next few seconds have replayed themselves a hundred times in slow motion through my mind. Spence turned, jumped, shot the ball. The ball hit the far side of the rim, bounced up a little, hit the near side, then bounced out. Josh blew the whistle and the game was over.

Even though we didn't feel like it, most of us went over to congratulate the Wildcats. Benjamin ignored them and went to get a drink.

"Good game," I told Bruce Maxfield.

"We'll have to do it again sometime," he panted. "Not too soon."

Bruce's dad was congratulating Donavan on the youth center team's performance.

"They do it all on their own. We don't really have a coach," Donavan said.

"Well, they can be proud of their showing today," Mr. Maxfield said.

Benjamin heard him and shot him an angry glare.

I know the players from Texaco were excited and proud

but they were too tired to do any gloating. We'd given them a good fight and maybe next time. . . . They realized the possibilities, too.

After they left, Donavan walked over to Benjamin. "Good game. You ought to be proud."

"Of losing?"

"Of playing so well, and hanging tough for the entire game."

"We could have won."

"It was a close fight, maybe next time. . . ."

Benjamin spat on the court. "Nelson messed us up. He should have passed the ball to me. I could have made the shot. No, like a fool, he passes to his white friend."

"Spence was closer to the basket," I said.

"I'm a better shooter."

Donavan rubbed his face with both hands, then said, "It doesn't help to pick that last play apart now. Who can say how it would have turned out if this had happened, or that had happened?"

"You're saying that because you're white like the player who lost the game for us."

Donavan looked hurt.

"I think that way, too," Josh said, "and, for sure, nobody would mistake me for white."

Some of the boys grinned but Benjamin just turned around and stalked off through the gate.

I followed him. "Hey, Benjamin, wait up!"

He didn't slow his pace and, when I finally came alongside, he wouldn't look at me.

"Slow down a little, *sik'is.*"

"I'm not your friend," he said without slowing.

When we started across the bridge where the highway crosses the river, I said, "Man, are you stubborn! I just want to talk a minute."

100

He stopped and whirled to face me. "Talk."

Now that I had his attention, I wondered what I could say. I started rambling. "I'm sorry we lost the game but, no matter what you say, you're my friend."

He snorted.

"I guess I just want to understand what makes you hate Spencer West so much. . . . He's a good person. . . . He likes you, heck, he likes everybody. . . ."

"You're so stupid, Nelson!" He wiped the sweat from his forehead. "I know the Gas and Goodies boy is a good person. Of all the whites I know, he's the only one I'd call good."

My mouth fell open.

"I don't hate Spencer West because he's white. I hate him because he's here, here in Carson's Crossing, at our school, at the youth center. He doesn't belong in those places. There are a million other places, better places than we can even imagine, for him and the other *Bilagaanas*."

He sat on the railing of the bridge. "You just don't get it, do you, Nelson? Everybody keeps pushing Navajos around. They give us a little part of the land we used to have, land that isn't good for anything, and they expect us to be grateful. When we can't raise food or start industries here to make jobs, they give us welfare, and they expect us to be grateful."

He rubbed his face with both hands. When he began again, his voice shook. "The only thing we had . . . *I* had was the youth center. It was a tiny part of the world that was mine. It was a place where they couldn't remind me that I wasn't good enough. Then, Spencer West showed up and took over."

His bottom lip quivered, and I looked toward the river. He'd never forgive me if I saw him cry.

In a minute, I said, "It doesn't have to be like that,

Benjamin. It isn't *us* and *them*. There's just us . . . people
. . . everybody.''

I looked over to find him staring at the river, too.

"The reservation isn't separate from the rest of the
world," I went on. "Navajos need to go out and take
their place in that world."

He sighed. "You really are stupid, Nelson," he said
tiredly. "They won't let you become a part of that world.
Look around you and think. Your father, my father, any
others that are making a place in the *Bilagaana* world—
they are only making that place where they are allowed
to make it."

Benjamin lifted his foot to the railing to tie his shoelace.
"When Spencer West gets tired of slumming and doesn't
want to be your friend any more, remember what I told
you about the world."

He turned and walked across the bridge and I let him
go. I had to think about some of the things he'd said.
They weren't true, but I'd never convince him of that.
Maybe I had to convince myself first.

Chapter Eleven

The following afternoon, I helped my mother with a jigsaw puzzle. If she was surprised when I slid a chair next to hers and started studying the mixed up pieces, she didn't show it.

Clearing my throat, I watched her snap a piece into place, then I studied the puzzle again. I wasn't really looking for matching shapes, I was working on a different puzzle.

When I cleared my throat again, Mom said, "Are you catching a cold?"

"I don't think so."

Yvonne's voice pushed through the silence of the kitchen, accusing Rosemary of having her things all over the bedroom. Then came Rosemary's usual response, "It's my room, too, Queen Yvonne." The volume of the Dodger's game on TV was low, but once in awhile a cheer or groan escaped from Russell and Dad. The refrigerator in the corner rattled to a stop, and the quiet in the kitchen became louder.

I started to clear my throat and caught myself.

"Something on your mind?" Mom placed another puzzle piece.

"I'm just trying to sort something out . . . make sense of something I heard yesterday."

"I'm listening."

She kept working on the puzzle as I told her the details of the game and then, what Benjamin had said.

"I've never thought about those things before, Mom. I've never felt out of place because I'm a Navajo."

The refrigerator clicked and started its loud hum as I finished.

My mother turned to me, holding a puzzle piece against her lips for a few seconds. "There is some truth to what Benjamin said. Some people decide whether others have any value on the basis of their skin, their clothes, how they talk. You can only hope, if you *want* those people to accept you, that they will take the time to get to know you as a person."

She looked back at the puzzle. "When your father first went to work at the Texaco plant, he was dependable and worked hard. Not to impress people, he's just that way. For a long time, he was known as *a good Indian*. If he didn't like that title, he never complained to me. He just kept being himself, making the most of his job . . . his skills. By the time he left and took over the station here in town, he was a good *man*."

She looked up to see if I understood the difference.

"The other problem Benjamin was talking about is also real. There is a feeling of hopelessness around the reservation. It is almost a circle. Hopeless, bitter people are not confident people. Going far from home to compete for jobs takes confidence.

"Benjamin gets many of his ideas from his father. His father is talking from his own experience. Charlie Nez would like to be a supervisor at the plant. He's been passed over many times because he drinks too much. He is disappointed and drinks more and that makes him undependable, so he is passed over again. Like I said, it is a circle.''

I sighed. "It's so depressing.''

She put her hand on my back and rubbed it lightly. "It isn't hopeless, *shiyazh*. Talk things over with Adelia when she comes back from school in a few weeks. She has a better view because she's lived away from here."

I stood up. "Thanks. I think I'll go draw for a while."

"Thanks for your help with this puzzle." She smiled. We both knew I hadn't put a single piece in place.

Benjamin didn't come to the youth center for over a week. When he finally showed up, he played basketball in a detached, I'm-all-for-myself kind of way. He didn't call for people to pass the ball to him, but when he got it, he didn't pass either. He kept it until he worked his way in to shoot. He was playing alongside us, but he wasn't part of the team.

We might have been able to smooth things over and start working together again, but Donavan introduced his *Get In Touch With Navajo Heritage* week.

"It's going to be great," he said as the boys looked longingly at the basketball court. "Come on, you guys, pay attention. You promised you'd give me a few minutes to explain my plan."

We turned back to him.

"Next month, for one whole week, we'll try to get Carson's Crossing excited about Native American traditions."

I looked around at the others. The girls were smiling, glancing slyly at one another. For sure, Donavan hadn't hatched this plan by himself. Good old Walks Like A

Bear was the only boy who showed any interest at all. He didn't know any better.

"We'll fill the rec hall with displays that show the beauty of Navajo culture," Donavan went on. "Every evening from five to eight, we'll feature a local artist demonstrating Navajo arts and crafts—silversmithing, weaving, sandpainting, pottery, and any other arts we think of." He held his hands up in front of him as though he were holding back our applause. "Then, on Saturday evening, we'll have a big pow-wow, hire singers from over at Red Mountain, invite local tribal leaders to speak."

The excitement in his eyes diminished a little as all the guys just sat there.

He stood up. "Well? What do you think? If that doesn't spark some Indian pride, I don't know what will."

"How about paying people fifty dollars a day to wear badges that say, 'I'm Navajo and darned proud of it!'?" Benjamin suggested with a grin.

Freeman laughed. "Fifty dollars would spark my pride."

Donavan didn't smile. "Some of you spend a lot of time talking about how great it is to be Navajo. It's time to put forth a little effort to show that you really mean it."

Everyone looked at Benjamin. In a few seconds he shrugged. "Why not? We've got pride so we might as well show it."

His support pumped a little enthusiasm into the group. After a few minutes of thinking, we started brainstorming to get a list of things we could do to get the whole community involved.

In the middle of the discussion, Spence suggested, "We could advertise on Cedar Fort's radio station."

As Benjamin turned and stared at him, the group got quiet. "What about our Gas and Goodies boy?" he said. "He's not a part of Native American culture. He doesn't have any Navajo heritage."

Donavan paused a second, then shrugged. "Neither do Josh and I, but the three of us live here. We can still be proud of the traditions of the area."

Spence nodded. "Right. We're teammates. I'm proud of the traditions of my friends."

"What friends?" Benjamin said softly to Freeman in Navajo. They both looked over at me and laughed. "Most of us have better sense."

Nothing could dampen Donavan's exhuberance. He made us sit there for ten more minutes while he wrote down all our ideas before he'd let us play ball.

The next week, we had another meeting to report how plans were moving ahead.

"We have most of our artists lined up," he said. "Nelson's grandmother is going to demonstrate weaving on my loom. . . ."

"She is?" I said. At least his loom would get some use.

He nodded. "Benjamin's uncle, a silversmith, is doing things with turquoise jewelry."

A woman was coming to show the whole process of making pottery, from collecting clay to painting the finished pot. Another would show how baskets were made.

"The demonstration for the last night will either be making moccasins or sash belts. I'm waiting to see which person agrees to come first."

"Why not have both?" Spence suggested. "Just set them up in different parts of the room."

"That's a good idea. If any of you know other artists who might want to participate, we can have more than one demonstration going on at a time."

He reached for the folder sitting next to him on the grass. "We also need some displays that show various aspects of Navajo life. These pictures will give you an idea of what I mean." He slid some photographs out of the folder and started passing them around. I looked over Alex's shoulder. The picture looked familiar. When he handed it to me I understood why. It was one of the pictures Spence had taken on shearing day at Grandma's house that had caused so much trouble.

"Where did you get these?" Spence asked.

"I was talking to your mother about the program and she happened to have these handy," Donavan explained. "It's all right to use them in a display about raising sheep, isn't it?"

Spence was slow in answering.

"Why not?" Benjamin said. I couldn't tell if his grin was honest or sarcastic. "It's the first time Spencer tried to become a Navajo."

Apparently, Spence decided to treat the grin as friendly. "I almost sacrificed a sheep in the attempt." He laughed.

In a moment Donavan said, "If you have other ideas for displays or pictures, share them with us so we can arrange things that will really show Navajo life."

The memory of Felix and Myra kept gliding through my mind. "You know, Donavan, weaving, making moccasins, even sheep . . . all that stuff isn't really Navajo life, at least not the way it is now."

"You're right, of course. We all know that, but the idea behind the celebration is to let people who once lived that way remember it for a few hours and share

108

that way of life with people who will never get a chance to live it.''

Josh, who had walked up behind us, began clapping. ''Sounds good to me.''

When the week for the *Get In Touch* program finally arrived, Grandma was scheduled for the first night. Donavan's loom had been strung for weeks and she came in early in the afternoon to work on it for a few hours.

''The first part isn't very interesting,'' she explained to Donavan and Josh. ''It's better to show weaving after you have some of the pattern on the loom.''

Everyone had been working for a week, making sure the center sparkled from top to bottom and setting up bulletin boards and displays. I've got to admit the place looked impressive. We stood around on Monday afternoon feeling proud of our hard work.

''You kids had better get home and grab something to eat,'' Donavan said. ''Try and be back here at five. You're the hosts for this event. Make sure everybody feels welcome and comfortable. Just take them around to see all the displays and answer questions like we've rehearsed.''

We started moving out of the rec hall.

''Spence,'' Donavan called, and we waited. He walked over and put his hand on Spence's shoulder. ''How about taking pictures of the demonstrations and displays so we can document this program? The newspaper in town said they might be interested in an article about the project. With pictures, they may be even more interested. Who knows? This might turn into an annual event.''

''Pictures of the displays will be no problem,'' Spence said, looking over at me, ''but some people don't like to have their photographs taken, so I'll have to talk with each artist. I'll only take pictures of those who don't mind.''

"Good idea. I'll donate some money for film," Donavan offered.

"That's okay, I've got lots of film."

As we walked out, Spence called back, "I might take you up on a donation for getting the pictures developed though."

"I won't forget." The VISTA worker's voice followed us outside.

Every artist was willing to have pictures taken of their demonstrations. My grandmother was the most flattered of all.

"I just hope I don't become too famous," she told Spence with a teasing grin. "I don't want to travel all over the world showing people how to weave."

The place was crowded that first night, not surprising when you consider that the kids who hung around the Navajo Youth Center were related to almost everybody in Carson's Crossing. What amazed me was the number of people who came who I hadn't seen before, Navajo and white. Maybe Spence's idea about the radio station announcement had worked.

The camera's flash was really lighting up my grandmother when Benjamin finally arrived. I'd been too busy to notice he wasn't there. He took one look at Spence playing photographer and rushed over.

"What do you think you're doing?" he said angrily, grabbing Spence by the arm and pushing him across the room and outside. Spence was so surprised he didn't even resist.

I followed them.

"What are you talking about?" I heard Spence ask as I came out the door.

"For your information, *Bilagaana* boy who's so full of

110

cultural pride, a lot of Navajos don't like their pictures taken, especially older people.''

''I know that.''

Benjamin laughed. ''But you go right ahead and take pictures. You guys are all the same, you start pushing people around with no thought of their feelings.''

Spence laughed and Benjamin raised his fists.

''Whoa, Benjamin, just cool down.'' Spence held his hands up. ''I wasn't laughing at what you said.'' He laughed again. ''I was laughing because you were talking about white men pushing people around, and I thought of how I got outside.''

Benjamin had to smile. He let his hands fall to his sides.

''I'm trying to tell you that I *did* ask the artists if they wanted to have their pictures taken. Every one of them gave their approval. In fact, they want copies of the photos for themselves. I guarantee I'll ask each artist every night of the program.'' Spence folded his arms. ''Give me a break, *sik'is*. I'm not stupid.''

Benjamin might have commented on that but another voice broke through the dark, a Navajo voice. ''He's right, *shiyazh*. The young white man is not stupid.'' My grandmother stood at the door.

Benjamin looked at the ground.

''And you are not stupid,'' Grandma went on. ''I have known your family all my life. Your grandmother and I went to boarding school together. I have watched you grow from the time you were a baby on a cradle board, through many years to tonight. Here you stand, a handsome young man.''

She walked over and looked into his face. ''I'm going to tell you something about the world. Listen with your heart as well as your ears,'' she said in Navajo. Her voice was soft.

111

"The world is bigger than Carson's Crossing. It is bigger than the Navajo reservation and the United States. And the world is full of people, all kinds of people."

She folded her arms. "Whether a person is good or bad or a mixture has very little to do with the color of their skin. It is the heart that is in charge of good and bad, and every man's heart is the same color."

Benjamin put his hands on his hips and tapped his boot on the sidewalk.

"Don't be impatient, I'm almost finished. Your father is a good man, Benjamin, but I have known Navajos who were not. Spence is a good man, but I have known white men who were not."

She put her hands on Benjamin's shoulders. "You are old enough now to look beyond the outside appearance of things.

"Tonight you looked at Spencer taking pictures and saw things in a false way. Looking only at the outside of a person leads you to see him in a false way, too. You do not have to like Spencer West, but you must find better reasons not to like him than the way he looks on the outside."

Benjamin was no longer tapping his foot.

"Think about what I've said, *shiyazh*. It is true." Grandma gave his shoulders a pat, turned and walked back in to finish her demonstration.

Spence and Benjamin and I looked at one another for a few seconds. Then Benjamin turned and went into the dark.

Once again, he stayed away from the center for a few days. On Saturday, he came to the pow-wow and stood alone against the wall, watching the dancers but talking to no one.

Chapter Twelve

Summer in Carson's Crossing is hot. Midday air is like the inside of a car that's been parked in the sun all afternoon with its windows rolled up. About the only way to cool off, other than staying inside with the air conditioner turned to high, is to swim in the river. No one actually *swims* in the river because it's too shallow in most places. But we float along, sometimes in old inner tubes, with the current, scraping our backsides on rocks every few feet. Most years, by the end of July, rocks are sticking up through the muddy trickle like sleeping, dry-backed turtles. Then, even scooting with the current is impossible, but the river fills up again with the rains in August.

By the middle of June that year, unusual rains falling somewhere far away had kept the water deep, deeper than I'd ever seen it. Lots of trash and debris had washed down: limbs and weeds, tires, even a fifty-gallon oil drum. The river changes all the time. A place that's deep one day may become shallow by the next morning. The muddy water makes it impossible to see the bottom. It's no place to show off your fancy dives. All of us knew that.

The heat of summer had seemed to warm Benjamin almost to his heart. He was back on the team and on

Saturday morning, we all went to the youth center to play basketball. The heat was scorching by eleven but we hated to quit. Benjamin wanted to keep at it until his team won even though the sweat was rolling off us. Finally, we knew it was break for lunch or die. We chose lunch.

Afterward we came back, but our energy had evaporated with our sweat. We were content to lie around on the grass under the cottonwood trees.

"It's too hot to play ball now," Freeman said.

"Yeah, we should go swimming," I said.

I convinced them just that fast. We raced home, got our suits and went back to the river. In the hot afternoon air, we changed into our trunks, then hurried into the water. There was the usual splashing and pushing and shouting, "Geronimo!" Finally, we started to relax, sitting close to the bank on the rocky bottom with water up to our necks.

Our regular swimming spot is a wide place in the river, deeper than the rest. Not twelve feet or anything but deep enough that you can swim across it without scraping your hands on the bottom as you paddle. The place is shaded by cottonwoods and bordered by big sandstone rocks along the bank.

"Did you see the sports special last Sunday on cliff divers in Mexico?" Spence asked me.

"Just the last of it," I said. "Pretty brave, aren't they?"

"Who's brave?" asked Benjamin, floating in on the last of our conversation.

"Cliff divers from Mexico," I said. "They get up on the cliffs and dive a hundred feet into the ocean."

"They have to time their dive just right," Spence added. "If the waves are out, they'll crash on the rocks."

"The wind has to be right, too."

114

"Sounds like fun to me," Benjamin said.

As we floated in silence for a few seconds, I watched him study the big rocks at the edge of the bank.

"Hey, Spencer," Benjamin said at last, "I dare you to dive off that rock over there."

"No way, Benjamin. Around here, you can never tell where the bottom of the river is."

"Come on, chicken," sneered Benjamin. "Let's see who's braver, whites or Navajos."

"Forget it. You might just find out who's the deader."

"I can do it," Benjamin boasted.

"Just forget the whole thing," I said. "It's too dangerous."

"I'm no chicken." Benjamin headed for the bank.

"Nobody called you a chicken," Spence said tiredly. "Nobody's a chicken. Just forget it."

"Hey, you guys," yelled Benjamin, splashing his way through the last few feet of shallow water. "Watch this. You are about to see *Benjamin, the Great*."

The others turned toward him.

"Come on, Benjamin. Knock it off," I said.

He pulled himself up the side of the largest rock, then slowly stood up until he teetered unsteadily at the top.

"Cliff diver!" he shouted.

Spence said, "Benjamin, don't be such a dope."

That was the wrong thing to say. Benjamin stood tall. "Did you guys hear what the Gas and Goodies boy called me? A dope! Well, watch this, Smells Like A Bear."

He wobbled for a second or two, then dove into the river. His footing had not been the best and the dive was terrible. It was shallow enough but it veered off toward the bank. I didn't worry. The worst that could happen was a skinned stomach.

Everyone waited. No Benjamin. We started over toward

115

the spot he had entered the river. Suddenly, his foot appeared, kicking frantically above the muddy water. Then, Benjamin's left hand splashed to the surface.

Spence lunged toward it. "Come on, you guys! He must be caught on something."

Spence grabbed Benjamin's foot and pulled but the diver stayed below the surface. Finally, my friend took a breath and followed Benjamin's body under the water. He reappeared with a piece of baling wire in his hand.

"Help me, you guys. Pull this wire. Move fast!"

Some of us were on the bank now, using the traction of solid sand instead of the slick river bottom. In what seemed like slow motion, we acted out a tug-of-war with the mysterious muddy river. Inch-by-inch, the river gave up the wire and Benjamin surfaced. He wasn't struggling now, just floating there. Spence pulled him close to the bank where we could haul him up on the wet sand. The baling wire was still wrapped around his right arm and shoulder.

When we flopped him on his back and I saw his blue lips, I knew it was too late. But Spence scrambled up on shore and pushed us out of the way. He pinched Benjamin's nose and pulled his head back, just like we learned in health class. He put his mouth over Benjamin's and gave two quick breaths. Benjamin's chest and stomach came up. Spence pushed gently on his stomach and then quickly turned him on his side as Benjamin vomited a mixture of muddy water and his lunch. I caught myself thinking, he had bean burritos for lunch just like me. It was gross, but Spencer cleared Benjamin's mouth with his fingers, put his own mouth over it and kept blowing into him every few seconds. Finally, the rest of us began to wake up.

116

"Freeman," I said. "Go call the E.M.T.s at the Texaco plant."

Freeman and Cecil ran off toward the gas station. Spence just kept blowing and counting. Finally, Benjamin gave a sputter, followed by a cough. He tried to push Spence away, struggling to sit up, coughing a little stronger. Then, he rolled over and vomited again. After a few more coughs, he opened his eyes and looked around.

The first thing he saw was Spence, old Walks Like A Bear. His eyes widened but he didn't say anything. For what seemed like a long time he just lay there, his face changing from a bluish color to a sick white. By the time the ambulance came, he was sitting up and we had the wire off his shoulder. The E.M.T.s made us step back while they checked him over. Although he seemed all right, they loaded him into the ambulance and took him to the Public Health Service Hospital in town.

The crowd that had followed the ambulance stood around watching it pull away.

"That was really something, Spence," I said at last, patting him on the back.

The others nodded.

He looked at the ground. "It wasn't anything the rest of you wouldn't do. I just got to him first."

All of us knew that we had been bumble heads but we were glad he didn't bring it up.

If this were the movies, the next scene would show Benjamin walking out of the hospital to find Spencer West waiting. They would shake hands and end up best friends. But Carson's Crossing is a long way from Hollywood. We don't have many miracles around here. People don't change as fast as that.

Benjamin did get out of the hospital the next day. They

117

only kept him for observation. But he was still the old familiar Benjamin Nez.

He might have changed a little, but any major overhaul is going to take lots of time. Today, I was sitting on the grass at the youth center behind him and his friends when Spence walked through the gate.

Freeman said, "If you let *Bilagaanas* into a game, even one time, you never get rid of them."

Benjamin just looked at Spence. "Shut up, Freeman," he said, "that one's okay." He stood up and stretched. "You shouldn't judge things by the way they look on the outside."

As he walked over to meet Spence on the court, he added, "Anyway, the team needs him."

I walked down to the river after the game to sketch the spot where Benjamin performed his crazy cliff diving stunt. Branches and cans and other debris were still floating down.

Abandoning my sketch pad, I picked up a stick and threw it into the muddy water. It bobbed and twirled with the current, finally nudging against brush that was wedged into the rocks. The force of the water pushed it upright just like the smooth stick that Spence had thrown into the river coming home from school on the first day we met. This new stick stood against the flow until a branch floated in to give it support.

If it fights against the current long enough, I thought, maybe the stick will add a few more twigs and leaves, then another branch, and another. Maybe debris will keep swirling in, adding to the snag until the flow of the water changes a little.

I didn't stay to watch.

A Glossary of Navajo Words

Before listing individual words with their meanings, maybe a literal translation of the three complete sentences used in the book would be interesting. You might get a glimpse of some of the structure of the Navajo language.

Ya'at'eeh—Hello
kl'izi—goat
sani—old.

Notice that adjectives usually follow nouns in Navajo.

Dibe—Sheep
bichaan—its droppings
Biligaana—white man
bith—with him
thlikaan—it is tasty

Verbs generally come at the end of a Navajo sentence.

Kl'izi choon—Billy goats
ayoo—extremely
da—(plural marker)
nith—with them
choon—there is stink

No wonder I'm still studying Navajo! It's fascinating!

Bilagaana—an Anglo, a white person

hagoone—goodbye

iniyaa'ish—have you eaten?

kl'izi sani—old goat

shimasani—my grandmother (on mother's side of family),
        also a title of respect for an older woman

shiyazh—my son (when a mother is talking)

sik'is—my friend (of the same gender, female to female
        or male to male)

ya'at'eeh—hello (translates: "it is good")

yai!—an expression used when you're surprised or startled

yinishye—I am named